DRIVEN BY HER LESBIAN BOSS

K.F. JONES

"You missed a bit," Mistress Susanna said, pointing with her left hand as she sipped her tea with her right.

Amber looked at the spot on the wall and ran her roller over it a few times, the whitewash splashing into the cracks, and little sprays of it splattering everywhere. She wondered if she'd have made the same suggestion again, in hindsight.

"Is that better, Mistress? This whitewash is messy stuff," Amber said.

"It's not whitewash, my girl. It's masonry paint, far tougher for cleaning," Mistress Chevalier corrected her.

"Fine, is the masonry paint now covering the bit I missed, Mistresses," Amber said with an audible sigh.

Vicky gasped, but didn't stop her own smooth action with the paint roller she held. Ginger giggled, but very quietly.

"Yes, you got it and don't be so cheeky, Amber," Mistress Susanna said.

"I'm sorry, Mistress," Amber replied.

Mistress Susanna nodded curtly and set her tea down, picking up a piece of chalk and adding a tally mark to Amber's column. Amber winced. That was another punishment she was due. At least she was still behind Pepper.

When they'd begun the preparation work on the stable buildings, Amber had envisioned it being much easier. After all, a little planning and some negotiation with the builders had allowed them to keep the cost of the professional work down, if Susanna and her staff could manage to do some of the simpler elements of the labour.

The building that hadn't been refurbished yet was filthy and full of junk of one form or another. First, they'd had to clean out old straw and muck, clean up decades of dirt and pull out rotten stable doors and woodwork. Much of what they'd had to take out was disposed of fairly easily. Some in skips, some on bonfires and some to a scrap metal dealer.

They'd found a number of things that needed to be restored because they were antique. Some beautiful cast iron boot scrapers, for instance, that were currently with a professional restorer to bring them back to their former glory.

Today was the last thing they were doing for at least a while before the contractors moved in. Just a couple of coats of whitewash, or rather, masonry paint, before they were done. Mistress Susanna and Mistress Chevalier sat in old, wooden farmhouse chairs watching the girls work.

Susanna's ponygirls, Ginger and Pepper were helping and Mistress Chevalier's ponygirl, Vicky was there too. At some point or other, all of Susanna's staff of submissive lesbians had pitched in to tidy up, but now it was just them.

Pudding couldn't help all the time if they all still wanted good meals, for instance. Roxy was off driving people around for Susanna's business, a task she clearly didn't relish. The maids were doing their bit keeping the main house tidy, or rather the private areas for which they alone were responsible.

That left Amber and the ponygirls, the warm spring air, painting the stable walls with rollers and brushes. It might end up being painted over by professionals, which made it a little frustrating, but if it went well, it could save a lot of time and money.

The girls were all naked, which Mistress Susanna had ordered to ensure they didn't get their clothes dirty. Or at least, that was what she'd said, with a twinkle in her eyes that suggested to Amber that their Mistress wasn't averse to making them work in the nude for her pleasure. Mistress Chevalier had seemed to think it was a good idea too.

Ginger and Pepper had been keen that they should wear their tails while they worked and had asked if they could. Mistress Susanna had immediately refused, saying she didn't want the paint getting on the 'hair' that made up the tails as it wouldn't be easy to wash off.

Mistress Chevalier had found a compromise that Ginger, Pepper and Vicky were keen to accept. A few silicone butt plugs with curly tails had been produced and were soon inserted in the ponygirls. They weren't for ponies, but for little pigs, but they were equally filling.

Amber tried politely to decline wearing one as well, but Susanna had ordered her to be plugged the same as the others. When Amber tried to back away, Susanna ordered her seized and held down. Vicky had taken great pleasure in holding her still, while Ginger and Pepper slowly lubricated her bottom and finally filled it with a plug. It felt much larger than the ones that the others had more willingly bent over to receive.

"Ow. That's so big," Amber had protested, with a rather whiny tone.

"That's what you get when you're bratty, my girl," Mistress Chevalier said.

"Yes, it certainly is. If you behave yourself, you'll get the same treatment as the good girls," Mistress Susanna had agreed, without sympathy.

"It's only an inch or so more circumference and you took it easily enough, don't pout so much," Mistress Chevalier had said, before Amber was ordered to get to work.

Amber moved back to the section she had been working on before she was told she'd missed a patch, and dipped her roller back in the tray, before lifting it up toward the ceiling and beginning a long roll down the wall. The refreshed roller spattered and dripped quite a bit, because she'd let it pick up too much paint.

"Hey! Mind what you're doing," Ginger protested, as the paint speckles splashed against her skin.

"Yeah, watch it Amber, you're getting it everywhere," Pepper agreed, wiping at the mess on her arm.

"It's just paint, it'll come off in the shower," Amber said with a heavy sigh.

"Oh, ok then, if it'll come off in the shower, that's alright," Ginger said with the kind of withering sarcasm that only the English can summon. Ginger picked up one of the smaller brushes, dipped it in her paint tray, and then flicked it at Amber, splattering the cold white paint across her breasts and belly.

"Oi!", Amber squealed, shaking her long handled roller above Ginger's head, causing yet more paint to be splashed around over the girls.

Pepper squealed as she was splashed again and got her revenge by running her roller up Amber's thigh, leaving a big white streak up her leg.

Ginger tried to flick her brush again, but this time her aim was off, and the paint splattered over Vicky's muscular back and bottom. The tall, athletic woman rounded on the rest of them and growled. At the party Susanna held a few weeks ago, Amber had heard several of the women refer to Vicky as 'The Amazonian' and the nickname wasn't inaccurate. Vicky was tall but also had the kind of figure that came from bodybuilding or weightlifting. There were defined muscles pretty much everywhere you looked, and Amber knew from experience that wrestling her was a losing proposition.

Vicky advanced on Ginger and pinned her quickly against the wet paint on the wall, before swatting her on the bottom with a large paintbrush. "Watch what you're doing!" Vicky rumbled as she punished the smaller woman.

Ginger wriggled, but Vicky kept her against the wall with no apparent effort. Amber could see her breasts were squashed against the wet paint, but despite Ginger's verbal protests, her mouth was curled in a lusty smile as she enjoyed being overpowered by the larger ponygirl.

"Enough!" Mistress Chevalier called out finally, as Pepper and Amber tried to get more paint on each other.

"Break it up, girls. There's work to do today," Mistress Susanna demanded. "Now!" she barked when the squabbling girls didn't immediately obey.

Finally, the girls calmed down and put their tools down.

"To the showers, now!" Mistress Susanna said sternly.

The two dominants marched them off to the shower room, and lined them up against the wall where they were made to wait, while the two dominants left the room. Vicky looked at the shower heads expectantly, but Pepper shook her head dejectedly.

"No such luck," Ginger whispered. "We won't get the showers for this."

Amber frowned, wondering what was going on. Clearly Susanna wanted them clean again, so presumably soap and a shower was just the ticket?

When Susanna and Jade came back, they were hauling a garden hose reel which Jade played out behind her. A bright yellow pressure nozzle was attached to one end, and Mistress Susanna looked cross.

"Face the wall, you filthy girls," Mistress Susanna ordered.

Everyone turned around and then the hose splashed against the wall. Amber squealed at the cold water splashing off the surrounding wall, and she wasn't the only one who flinched. The flow was adjusted from a narrow jet to a wide spray mode that was more like a powerful shower.

Then the water was played across their shoulders, back and forth, as Susanna got them all wet, and not in the way any of the submissives generally preferred. The water was cold. It was a sunny day, which was a mercy but it was still only spring so the mains water wasn't anywhere near lukewarm though thankfully it wasn't as icy as it would have been in the winter.

The girls were all shivering in short order as the water washed over them, and Susanna moved back and forth over them, making sure all the paint was washed off. Then it was time to turn around.

"Wash your faces," Susanna ordered, and while they did that with the cold water that dripped down their bodies, she ran the hose over their breasts, pummelling their tender flesh and washing away the drops of paint. As the girls squealed and yelped at the cold water which made their skin produce goose-bumps, Susanna adjusted the flow back to a narrow jet which she used to target the worst areas, like Amber's well painted thigh.

When it was at last done, and each girl was inspected, before being given one more rinse off with the spray setting, they were allowed to move into the locker area, where large fluffy towels allowed them to get dry and a bit warmer.

They weren't given much time, and Amber was the last to dry off. She was still quite damp when they were all ordered back to work, chastened and feeling far less boisterous.

Amber heard Mistress Susanna saying something on the phone, and then the dominants returned to their chairs.

"I don't want to see any more displays like that, you naughty sluts," Mistress Susanna said. "I want this done before it gets dark so get cracking."

A short while later, Amber was feeling warm again as she methodically painted the walls and all the girls cooperated with each other this time.

Then Sugar and Candy arrived, and her concentration was dealt a blow as she heard Mistress Chevalier and Mistress Susanna remove their trousers and sit down to have the submissive maids pleasure them. The wet sounds of passion behind them were a distraction Amber could do without. A warm glow started between her legs as she imagined being involved with the fun, either on her knees, or being worshipped by Sugar or Candy.

By the time they finished with their painting, and were allowed to turn around and see what was happening, Sugar and Candy, still in their revealing and wildly impractical, French maid uniforms, were just as hot and sweaty from their work, as Amber, Ginger, Pepper and Vicky were from the painting.

Amber coughed politely, "I think we're finished, Mistress."

Susanna looked up and shuddered as she tightened her grip on Candy's hair, inspecting the work. Apparently satisfied, if not by the approach of what Amber thought would be her third orgasm, at least by the painting, she nodded.

"Very well, go and wash off the brushes and rollers, put everything away, and you can all go back to the house to get ready for dinner," Mistress Susanna ordered.

"Yes, Mistress," the girls chorused.

CHAPTER 2

"Now, Amber, can you name all these items correctly?" Mistress Chevalier asked.

Amber looked at the assortment presented on the table in the newly finished stable building. The last of the contractors had left the day before, and Mistress Susanna hadn't wasted any time in bringing her out this morning for her first training session.

"Bridle, reins, boots obviously, body harness, and a bit gag? Then there are the ears, a tail, and blinders," Amber replied, touching each item as she named them. Having had next to no riding experience as a kid, Amber was happy with her performance.

Mistress Chevalier had given her some reading material as homework to study up on while the contractors were in, so it wasn't a work of any particular genius, but she was happy that she got everything right.

"Good. It's important that you learn the terminology so you can get dressed yourself, and help other girls get dressed, too," Mistress Chevalier said.

"We'll dress you this time, you can consider this a taster session. Often, the submissives present themselves attired properly for our pleasure," Mistress Susanna added.

"Yes, that's a popular way to do it. I enjoy scenes where I get Vicky ready, strip her down naked, put her in her tack and harness, and then give her rub downs and hair brushing after a scene. You must learn how to satisfy whichever dominant you're playing with, and their particular needs, of course," Mistress Chevalier said.

Amber nodded as the two older women instructed her, trying to absorb what they were saying, in case there were tests later. The taste she'd developed for the sweet caress of the cane didn't mean she wanted to experience it so regularly that failure held no fear for her.

It seemed better to do as well as she could, and then be punished or pleasured with Mistress Susanna's impact toys, as her domme felt necessary. Being cheeky or lax, just took the experience into the zone of true punishment, to be borne not revelled in.

"Yes, Mistress," Amber said when they'd finished talking.

The harness and bridle came first, then the ears and blinders. The boots were next, big, hoof-like platform heels that made her stand almost on tiptoes. They made a satisfying clopping noise against the floor of the tack room.

"Bend over that spanking bench, Amber," Mistress Susanna said calmly.

At first, Amber wondered if she was to be punished for something, but then Mistress Susanna fetched several butt plugs which had long tails hanging from them. Amber swallowed hard, as her domme matched the colours to her hair to make her choice.

"What do you think, Amber? Does this one look like it would suit you? The colour is the closest I have to your hair. If you do well, I'll get you something custom made, of course," Mistress Susanna purred enticingly.

"It does look quite big, Mistress," Amber pointed out.

"Yes, but that will help it stay in. It's such a drag when a new girl drops her tail out of her bottom. When you've been doing your exercises for long enough, that won't be a problem. You'll be able to grip it tightly for me, all day if I require," Mistress Susanna said.

"Yes, Mistress."

"What do you think, Mistress Chevalier? Is this too big for our new pony?"

The Stable Mistress came forward and inspected the butt plug in front of Amber, stroking the length and squeezing the girth. "I think she'll be able to take this with no problem. Perhaps she'll squeal a bit, but I'd be surprised if she doesn't cream up in a hurry when you put it in her. It's just this wide bit, Amber, that presents a challenge, but once it's pushed slowly and firmly into your bottom, your tight little rosebud will close behind it and you'll get used to it," Mistress Chevalier explained, as Amber's cheeks flushed at the thought of the impending intrusion.

"Would you mind doing the honours, Jade, while I tend to the bit gag?" Mistress Susanna asked.

"Happily," Mistress Chevalier replied, taking the plug behind Amber.

"Now, this gag goes in your mouth," Mistress Susanna explained, as strong fingers coated Amber's tight hole with lubricant and began to slide slowly inside her, slowly coating her ring with the cool gel.

Amber whimpered, but made an effort to relax as much as she could, to admit the intruding digits of Mistress Chevalier.

"When it's in, it'll be attached to your reins, and we can gently tug on it to make you turn your head and direct you. Do you understand, Amber?"

Amber nodded and her eyes went wide as a second finger plunged deep inside her. The squelching noises coming from her bottom echoed around the room, and she knew her chest and neck had a rising crimson flush. Amber also knew that Mistress Susanna was enjoying her sense of shame at being on display like this. It certainly wasn't going to elicit sympathy from her boss.

"Good girl. One stamp of your hoofs for yes, two for no, three for your safeword if something is too much. Got it," Mistress Susanna said, cupping her chin in her hand. "You won't be able to speak clearly around this, though you are free to scream and cry if you feel the need."

"Yes, Mistress," Amber managed, before the rubber bar was placed between her teeth and gently, but firmly pushed back into her mouth. Amber could tell that drooling was going to be a bit of a problem for her and that didn't help her sense of humiliation one bit as Susanna fastened the leather straps behind her head and adjusted the buckles until it was firmly in place. Then she attached the reins and experimentally tugged them, turning Amber's head to the left and right.

"Turn to the left. Turn to the right. Left. Right. Pulling up on both means stop. This flick of the reins, means go," Susanna explained.

Mistress Chevalier withdrew the three fingers she'd been working in and out of Amber's arsehole, and presented the well-lubricated butt plug instead, firmly pushing it inside her. It stopped, obstructed by the tight ring of muscle, and was withdrawn, only to be worked forward again.

The sensation was uncomfortable, humiliating and Amber knew, was making her sopping wet. As she grew more aroused, and more used to the wide intrusion, she imagined the plug was opening her up and being admitted further into her bottom. Then, with a squelch and a quite glorious sensation from her rosebud, it passed the widest point and her ring closed around the tapered section.

Mistress Chevalier mumbled something that sounded positive, then tugged it back and forth a few times to make sure it was properly in place. "I don't think that's coming out by accident, Mistress Susanna," she reported.

"As long as it comes out when we want it to, that's fine," Susanna replied.

"I find a wand against the clit for half an hour, tends to loosen them up a bit if they have trouble letting go," Mistress Chevalier said dismissing the problem. Amber gulped. A half hour of such play would leave her shattered and broken, those things were so intense. Amber wasn't sure if she should be terrified at the prospect or if she should hope she wouldn't be able to let go of the plug when the time came.

"Perhaps we should experiment one day? We have four ponygirls at the moment, if we count our new trainee that is," Mistress Susanna said.

"Oh yes, there's nothing more erotic than the scientific method being applied to a sexy young woman's bottom," Mistress Chevalier said with a filthy chuckle.

"I think Ginger would take the biggest one," Susanna remarked.

"Yes, but perhaps Vicky could hold on to one the longest. She's got muscles everywhere you know," Jade replied.

"I know they say it's important not to miss any muscle groups, big or small," Susanna said.

"As far as I've discovered, she doesn't."

Amber turned her head to the side where Vicky was waiting patiently, nude aside from her own harness, with Ginger and Pepper. All three ponygirls were in their full gear and had been getting the full show as Amber was dressed and penetrated. They seemed quite animated at the prospect of a butt plug competition, but in a way that suggested to Amber that they were looking forward to it, rather than dreading it. *They're all just as slutty as me, she thought to herself as her arousal ran down her thigh.*

Mistress Susanna interrupted her thoughts by taking a firm grip of a large brass ring that linked the straps of her harness between her shoulder-blades and hauling her upright bodily. With a moment or two to balance on the high platforms of the hoof boots, Amber found the butt plug was firmly in place and the tail swishing against her thighs.

"Walk on," Susanna ordered with a flick of the reins and slowly guided her out into the yard in front of the stables. Amber was grateful that the estate was so secluded. The front gate had to be at least half a mile from the front of the house, and the grounds were extensive. Amber felt a frisson of pleasure at the thought of being spied by someone out for a country walk, if they went to the edges of the estate, but there was no real risk this close to the house. Perhaps a naughty ponygirl might run off and visit the edges of the grounds, where the public footpaths might be found?

In the meantime, Amber had to walk around the yard, performing wheels and turns as instructed. Susanna began to teach her the basics of the gaits she was expected to use. Walking, trotting and cantering. Galloping wasn't something she wanted to get into on the first day.

After lunch, Mistress Chevalier, who had been observing during the morning, helped Mistress Susanna harness Amber to a small trap. It wasn't the same as the ones that Amber and Susanna had used for their race.

"Is this a different model, Mistress," Amber asked, grateful that the bit hadn't been replaced after lunch.

"Well spotted. It's a training model, lighter and flimsier than the ones the other day. It makes it easier for you to learn, and you'll use it the first time you try moving and pulling a passenger in the trap, or running at a good racing trot," Mistress Susanna said.

"Yes, there's no hurry, you'll get used to the various vehicles one at a time, with and without the weight of the passengers," Mistress Chevalier added. "Then you get to try it with a rider. That way, you don't get anyone injured, including yourself. Safety first!"

Amber had thought that would have been secondary, but since coming to know Mistress Susanna, she had been educated in the rigorous standards that BDSM players adhered to. Safewords were familiar to her already, from various books and films, but it wasn't until she began to serve Susanna that she'd understood.

Play was always to be safe, sane and consensual, Susanna had told her one night, early in their relationship. Whatever was to be done, the submissive must have consented, and precautions had to be taken to ensure their safety. Even simple bondage with rope could cause nerve damage, if the players were amateurish about it.

Plenty of videos she'd seen or books she'd read had featured subs and slaves being suspended from frames and ceilings with complete ease, but Susanna had laughed at such questions. Rope bondage took practice and time, and suspension was perfectly safe, but only if done correctly.

As Susanna had an impatient streak, she preferred padded leather cuffs and the like for bondage, and was more inclined to put Amber in a sex swing, than suspend her by her restraints.

The idea that safety came first, when she was likely to be disciplined with a cane or paddle later, and caused significant pain, would have seemed incongruous to Amber just a few short weeks ago. But now she had come to know that each implement required knowledge and skill to inflict pain, while minimising injury. A bruise healed well, but a split in the skin was a different matter.

Now, Mistress Chevalier's assertion that safety with the traps and carts in the stables was important, even though the abundance of whips and crops suggested a ponygirl would be regularly subjected to painful stimulus. Amber could expect that her bottom would be turned quite pink from a cropping or paddling if she misbehaved, but having a trap collide with a pony was something to be avoided. Deliberate punishment versus accidental injury.

"Yes, Mistresses, thank you for explaining."

Mistress Susanna had Amber walk around the yard pulling the light training trap behind her as she talked to her Stable Mistress. Every few laps, the order would go out for Amber to change gait or walk in a figure of eight rather than a circle, practicing manoeuvres.

Although the trap was very light and on good quality wheels, which appeared to be made from bicycle wheels, it was still quite a lot more exercise than Amber was used to doing. She was no gym bunny, by any means, and it was easy to see why Mistress Chevalier and the other dommes were so excited by the prospect of Vicky as a ponygirl.

Amber could well imagine the Amazonian competing on a TV game show about the hyper-fit, and crushing her enemies, seeing them driven from the field, and hearing the crying of their women, or men. Like a 1930s barbarian heroine.

As Amber practiced her gaits, the two dominants sat at a table that was sheltered from the bright sunshine by a large umbrella sticking up from the middle.

Susanna called for refreshments from the kitchen.

CHAPTER 3

"I'm surprised they got all that work done so quickly," Mistress Chevalier said.

"It doesn't hurt to have a good recommendation from a friend."

"They did an excellent job. I haven't found anything that doesn't work or fit or wasn't finished properly. Which is a far cry from every other time I've had to have a bathroom replaced or new light fittings, I can tell you," Jade said.

"I'm glad to hear it. It's worth paying for the best, but I don't know how I'd have found them without a referral."

"It was the Baroness who suggested the firm, yes? I should send her a thank you note."

"Yes, it was. I'm sure she'll be happy to be thanked at the next get together, but Amber can put a letter in the post for you if you want to write one," Susanna replied.

"That must be nice, having a personal assistant to take care of administrative work."

"Yes, I highly recommend it. I hope you can grow your business in your new workshop and then perhaps we can find you an Amber of your own?" Susanna replied.

Mistress Chevalier chuckled at that, "I love the sound of that. What type of girl should we look for?"

"How about a fashion student, who has just completed a degree in Leather for Fashion, at the University of Northam?"

"That's a thing, is it?"

"Yes, an absolutely genuine qualification."

"Now, how would you know that? I've been marking tack and harness for, well, some time now," Jade demurred, "and I didn't know there were fashion degrees based on leather."

Susanna answered coyly, "I may have done some research."

"Have you now?" Jade chuckled.

"Yes, there are all sorts of relevant qualifications, from the trades guilds in London and the various arts and fashion courses. To me it seems obvious that there are two types you might consider," Susanna opined.

"Do go on."

"Well, there are you art and craft types of people, who have studied the skills of working with leather for tack and harnesses and the like, perhaps for horses or more for human fashion. Then there are ones who've done metalwork or woodwork for other toys or for the metal parts of your gear," Susanna answered.

"That would definitely be helpful. It would save me a lot of time if the basic tasks could be handed off to an apprentice who already had skills," Jade agreed.

"The second type is those with more of a design and fashion background. They may have less in the way of practical skills at manufacturing your goods, but might be great at realising the designs you describe in the way the rest of the industry does. Either way, many of the higher level degrees and craft courses contain some basic level of business skills as well. What you need is a good all-rounder who can help with your website, sending out orders, construction of garments. Honestly, it doesn't matter which elements that you do, that your first employee takes off your hands. Your time is currently the most important asset you have," Susanna advised.

"I must say, we've only been moved in a few days, the flat still smells of fresh paint. But coming up to the main house for meals, and Sugar and Candy helping with the laundry has been invaluable," Jade said. "I suppose any hours I was spending doing something that I can put elsewhere are a massive boon."

"Exactly. People always assume it's the thing that only they can do that is most important. The computer coding, the artisan level craftwork, the generation of business ideas. In fact, it's the paperwork, stationery orders, responding to simple emails and the like, that takes up your bandwidth," Susanna said.

"It's going to be hard to find someone suitable, in any case, given my industry," Jade said.

"Not as hard as you think, but don't let Sugar and Candy take credit for the laundry. It all goes out to a very efficient service in the local village. They just gather it all up and take care of the simple things like towels. Nothing that requires ironing. I lost a number of good blouses to gardening duty that way. For the sake of your wardrobe and the environment, don't try to get them to deal with anything that requires a crease," Susanna said.

Jade laughed heartily at that. "The cheeky minxes didn't even hint at that. I thought they were the youngest people I'd ever met who knew how to use an ironing board properly."

"We'll add a few marks to their punishment tally then, because they definitely can't iron clothes properly," Susanna said. "The service will deal with dry cleaning items too, by the way, but nothing kinky. They're strictly vanilla."

"Noted. No peephole bras and the like," Jade giggled.

Susanna's nose wrinkled up at that, "Ew. Please tell me you don't have any of those. I've never seen one that wasn't tacky."

"No, I don't. Most of my obviously kinky items are leather so they're not going in a washing machine, don't worry," Jade said cheerfully. "It was the only thing I could think of, but I second your opinion. But you mentioned it might not be hard to find someone suitable, why not?"

"I have a good working system in place. You have to, in my position," Susanna said.

"I assume your HR department takes care of things like recruitment," Jade said.

"For the businesses I don't actually run myself, certainly," Susanna said. "But not for positions in my household. I have specialists for that."

"How do you mean?" Jade said, taking a sip of the freshly made lemonade that Candy and Sugar had brought out from the kitchen for them. The two maids were now helping Amber take a few sips with a long straw and giggling as she dribbled some past her bit.

"Finding someone like Amber, to work so closely with me, takes far more scrutiny than employing a night watchman for one of the factories," Susanna pointed out. "My specialists conduct more rigorous screening to ensure that I get the most likely candidates, and I never interview anyone who doesn't meet my requirements. I have to think they have a reasonable chance of fitting in for it to be worth my time."

Jade looked Susanna's latest employee up and down. Amber was pretty, beautiful even and given that the only clothing she currently wore consisted of thin straps of leather and kinky boots, and that she was being given a drink by two young women dressed as French maids, it seemed unlikely all that had been on the job advert.

"So Amber had been vetted somehow, before you met her?"

"Yes. I prefer to headhunt, because it gives me more time for checks to be done. But there are a series of steps we use. Firstly, we identify a broad pool of candidates who can do the work. In Amber's case, it was easy to find women who could do well as a personal assistant. It's a pretty board church and her duties are minimal," Susanna said.

"You must have a lot of people you have to reject. Men, for starters."

"I employ men, just not for personal service positions, for obvious reasons," Susanna replied. "In any case, most people don't know they're being vetted by a headhunter. Don't look at me like that. It's all above board and perfectly legal, we aren't breaching privacy, legally speaking. Believe me, the expensive kink friendly barristers I've had to employ have ensured that. Of course, if it's a job we are advertising, we get lots of applicants who aren't ever going to be ideal."

"Men?"

"Yes, men or people who have archaic views on human sexuality but might be excellent at the actual job. In which case, we do everything to find them a job somewhere in one of my companies that I don't ever actually have to meet them," Susanna explained. "I can't exclude a man from being my gardener, but I'm not required to employ sexists or homophobes. And the man has to be the most qualified candidate. Women's shelters don't have to employ men, for instance, and I don't object to male accountants. My driver is a woman because she's been diplomatic protection and was the most qualified driver I could find."

"Ok, ok. I get the point, you've dotted the i's and crossed the t's of equality law and you're not investigating people beyond the bounds of privacy laws either," Jade conceded.

"No, it's alright. It's an absolute minefield. But the short of it is that a few jobs where a woman, or a man, might be preferred, are permissible. A bra-fitter can be a woman, an actor for a female role can be, a man four counselling young boys who are traumatised, a gay man for talking to teenagers about coming out. That's all fine. But a cashier in a supermarket, that can be done by anyone. It's much more reasonable than you might think," Susanna said.

"Better than it used to be, though."

"Agreed. But regardless, positions in my household are reviewed by friendly legal experts before I try to fill them. Amber, for instance, is employed as a personal assistant," Susanna said. "If she turned out not to fulfil all the criteria, she would be working from an office in London and any visit she absolutely had to make here, would be fully managed."

"I see. How did you establish that she was suitable in all the ways you hope for, then?" Jade enquired.

"There are extensive psychometric tests that can reveal bad attitudes towards some groups, so that weeds people out. Then we look at legally available information. Like if they're married, part of a group that might give a clue and so on. We also ask people to volunteer their orientation on applications. All that can be done before the interview with me and I'm the last of several interviews," Susanna said.

"You can ask their sexuality? I honestly didn't know that," Jade replied.

"Yes, but they don't have to answer. We have excellent policies for supporting couples of all sexualities, and lots of people want their employer and colleagues to know these days," Susanna confirmed.

"That's so much better than the last time I had to apply for a job. It was very much don't ask, don't tell then."

"Anyway, that's it, basically. Before my team interview them, I discard any candidates that don't seem right, then they interview them and show my their shortlist. I might still discard someone then, when they've got more information to show me. After that, full background checks are done, and hopefully anyone I meet for an interview is suitable," Susanna said.

"Amber must have been," Jade said, curiously.

"Yes, that was a tricky one. There was nothing so blatant as being in the LGBT society at university, but there were some public social media posts, a few titbits here and there, that made us think she might have a healthy interest that was unexplored," Susanna winked.

"It seems like a fine line to walk though," Jade said.

"Let's just say that Amber's interview convinced me that we had correctly judged her, shall we?"

"Your silver tongue got the response that you needed to confirm your suspicions, then?"

"What a particularly apt way to put it," Susanna replied, provocatively licking her lips. "As for my silver tongue, it wasn't just my skills of persuasion that sealed the deal. One lick of a nipple, and I knew she was game for more."

"Susanna, you are so wicked!"

"You have to take the odd risk in life, now and then and Amber seemed like a worthwhile gamble, given all our preparation. You know, Jade, she barely hesitated to strip off in the napping room at my office so I could change her outfit," Susanna said. "That and the glances she'd been throwing me as I changed, were enough to make me throw caution to the wind and test her."

"I know I might seem bold, sometimes, but that's at nightclubs and such, where I know my targets are suitable. I don't think I could ever take a chance like that," Jade breathed.

"I don't think you'll have to; with the potential candidates you'd be looking for."

"What do you think that might be?"

"As I said, fashion graduates with an interest in leather," Susanna said coyly.

"The way you specified a university and a course earlier, I thought you had someone in mind already," Jade laughed.

"No, don't be silly."

"Of course not."

"I have five candidates for you look at," Susanna replied.

Mistress Chevalier's mouth dropped open at that.

"Amber, come here so we can get you unhitched. I want you to fetch a file from the office and bring it back for Mistress Chevalier," Susanna ordered.

"Yes, Mistress," Amber said.

CHAPTER 4

After the evening meal, Amber found herself being interviewed in Ginger and Pepper's flat. She'd been allowed to get out of her ponygirl harness and other gear, and was now more comfortably attired in a plaid micro-skirt, knee length white socks, and a tie up white crop top. No girl she'd ever been to school with dressed like that, but it was clearly the aim of the costume.

Amber had to keep her knees together to keep from flashing Mistress Susanna and Mistress Chevalier across the coffee table, as bra and panties weren't part of the outfit she'd been given. The ponygirls had been put to work moving some more of the equipment back down to the tack room. The flat had been full of dismantled benches, pillories, impact toys and the like, while the contractors were on site, on Mistress Susanna's orders.

The contractors were quite professional, polite and diligent and a surprising number employed by the firm, were women and at least a couple of the men were openly gay, which was a refreshing change from Amber's limited experience of builders and tradespeople.

They weren't to be exposed to anything in the slightest bit kinky though, not even the one or two who were quite likely lesbians themselves. "Just because they might be lesbians or gay, doesn't mean they're kinky, and even if they are, everything we do here is private," Mistress Susanna had explained. That was a perfectly reasonable point, Amber supposed. *Not everyone wanted to be exposed to sexuality at work, just because Amber was enjoying that, she thought.*

So, Amber sipped her tea delicately while the two dominants talked to her about her first day trying to play as a ponygirl. She confirmed that she had enjoyed it so far and found it interesting.

"Would you like to continue training then?" Susanna asked.

"Yes, please, Mistress."

"Good. We have talked and have a plan we'd like you to consent too. I have some business dealings coming up in London which will require me to be away for a week or so. During that time, we propose that Mistress Chevalier train you," Susanna said, holding up her hand to forestall questions. "Jade is, after all, the acknowledge expert here. If you agree, you will stay here for the full week."

"Yes. During that time, I will train you properly in all the basics, far beyond what you've learned during the introductory session today. By the time Susanna comes back, you'll be able to serve her as a ponygirl and she'll test your skills to see how you've taken to it," Mistress Chevalier continued.

"What would the training be, Mistress?"

"I will leave the specifics up to Mistress Chevalier of course, but you'll be taught about the equipment, racing traps, the common instructions and you'll practice everything until it's second nature," Susanna said.

"Yes, that's it. I will go through it with you in detail, of course."

"While I'm away, I would expect you to submit to Mistress Chevalier just as you do to me," Mistress Susanna said. "Just as you did at the party. I assume that won't be a problem for you?"

"You want me to please her sexually, Mistress?" Amber asked.

"Naturally. If Mistress Chevalier tells you to kneel, you will do so with good grace. If she tells you to bend over for a caning, you will do so gratefully. If she tells you to put your tongue to work on her pussy, you will do so with just as much diligence as I would expect where it me, demanding that you provide pleasure," Mistress Susanna said. "Again, is that an issue?"

Amber shook her head, "No, Mistress. I just wanted to be sure I understood correctly. I would be happy to stay here and learn about being a ponygirl and serve Mistress Chevalier for you."

"I'm glad to hear that. When I'm back, I will test your skills and see if you have the aptitude to be a ponygirl for me, like Ginger and Pepper. Are there any more questions?"

"What if I fail, Mistress? Will I lose my position here if I'm not a good ponygirl? I don't want to disappoint you, but what if I can't do it?" Amber asked nervously.

"Don't worry about that. I want you to try it. If you don't pass my tests though, you won't be dismissed. You'll still be my personal assistant and still be my submissive. I don't expect Sugar and Candy, or Pudding or Roxy to play this way, do I?" Susanna replied. "You will still be my girl. Now, do you want to play our games for the next week?"

"Please say yes, Amber. I guarantee I'll have a lot of fun with you," Mistress Chevalier said with a grin.

"Don't you mean, that I'll have a lot of fun, Mistress Chevalier?"

"Oh, possibly. I'll be exercising you hard though, every day, and you'll be disciplined for any misbehaviour or failure," Mistress Chevalier replied. "I'm sure some of it will be fun for you, but training you properly for your Mistress, and enjoying myself are my real concerns."

"Well, in that case, I can hardly say no, can I?" Amber said. "I consent to the training program."

"You can, but for forgetting to address us properly, you're going to get a spanking, young lady," Mistress Susanna snapped. "Over my knee, now."

"Yes, Mistress."

CHAPTER 5

By the time that Amber had received the dozen hard smacks on her bottom, that Mistress Susanna decided would be her punishment, she could tell her cheeks were glowing. She tried to look over her shoulder but couldn't see the resulting colour.

"Stand up and go to the mirror. See what you made me do to you, Amber," Mistress Susanna ordered. Amber complied, loving that her domme played into what she was trying to do.

Presenting her bottom to the full-length mirror that Ginger and Pepper had in their living room, she was able to see the effect the spanking had had on her pert cheeks. They were indeed glowing a most attractive shade of deep pink.

"What do you say after a spanking, Amber?"

"Thank you, Mistress, for correcting my behaviour."

"Good girl. Now, come back and wait here," Mistress Susanna said, pointing to a spot in front of the sofa that she and Mistress Chevalier were sitting on, before she stood herself and opened a cabinet next to the mirror.

Amber waited patiently as Mistress Chevalier looked her up and down, not bothering to conceal her appreciation of Amber's young, curvaceous body in the slightest. The Stable Mistress licked her lips as she admired the submissive before her. Amber could hear her Mistress getting ready with some kind of toy behind her, and she thought she knew what it was.

A few moments later, Mistress Susanna put a firm hand on Amber's shoulder. "On your knees, slut," she ordered, applying insistent pressure until Amber dropped to the floor, "now put your cheeky tongue to work for Mistress Chevalier. Show her how much your pussy eating has improved."

Mistress Chevalier smiled as she raised her bottom from the sofa cushion so she could hitch up her skirt, lowering herself at the edge of the seat to make her pussy available. Amber's tongue was soon slipping between her lips, and Mistress Chevalier's fingers twined into her hair, forcefully taking control of her. Having the older woman directing her attention as she wanted sent a thrill of pleasure down Amber's spine, raising goose bumps on her flesh.

Behind her, Amber heard Mistress Susanna drop a cushion on the floor and kneel down. The bulbous head of a dildo pressed against her wet lips, and her Mistress took a grip on Amber's hips, before slowly thrusting the strap-on into her submissive's pussy.

Amber moaned into Mistress Chevalier's pussy, enjoying the sensations of her pussy being filled as she tasted the older woman's lips. The way that the domme twisted her hair, tugged at her scalp just hard enough to make it clear who was in charge and be a little uncomfortable, which Amber found intoxicating.

"I think she's loving this, Susanna," Mistress Chevalier said, her voice thick with lust.

"I'll have to remember to pull her hair more often."

"Yes, it seems to be motivating her well. Her skills are certainly coming along nicely, aren't they?"

"I'm happy to say she's a quick learner, she's taking this cock well," Mistress Susanna agreed. "Her participation is much better than her first tries, she's pushing back properly and getting her hips where I need them, aren't you dear?"

Amber replied, but her words were muffled because Mistress Chevalier had no intention of letting her tongue leave her clit, just to let her speak clearly. "I think that was a yes. Lick me harder, slut, I want to come on that pretty face," Mistress Chevalier urged.

Complying wasn't a chore by any means, Amber was happy to do as instructed, revelling in the effect her tongue and lips were having on the older woman. Being able to please a domme who had doubtless had dozens of submissives bring her pleasure, and be complimented for her skills, was truly gratifying for her.

Amber's whole world was still in flux, all this was still new to her. Submitting to the whims of a lover, being disciplined with pain, restrained and shared with others were all revelatory experiences to her. Everything had happened so fast, and less than six months ago, she could never have imagined being in this situation.

Being on her knees between two lovers was certainly a fantasy that she'd had, but the Amber of six-months ago, couldn't have imagined that she would actually do that one day soon. Nor could she have honestly said that she might be in this position, between two women.

Her first proper lesbian experiences had been with or under the instruction of Susanna. Amber knew that Mistress Chevalier had had her first experiences before she was even born, and to be able to bring her to orgasm was a delight.

True to her word, when Mistress Chevalier began to come, Amber's face was made as wet as her she could feel her pussy was. The older woman ground her wet pussy into Amber's mouth, and when her spasms subsided, she rolled her hips. Mistress Chevalier rubbed Amber's face against her hot, wet pussy, smearing her juices all over the young submissive's chin, lips and nose. Amber was left gasping and struggling desperately, trying to get her tongue back to work.

Mistress Chevalier's hand pushed her away from her sensitive nub, "Enough, slut. You've had more than enough."

"If she wants more pussy, shall we swap places?" Mistress Susanna suggested.

"More than happy to, though I'm a bit weak at the knees, I'm sure I'll recover in a minute or two," Mistress Chevalier said, pushing Amber aside and standing unsteadily.

Mistress Susanna pulled back, withdrawing the long, thick silicone cock from her submissive's aching pussy, then unstrapping it and passing it to her friend.

Amber's tongue was soon lapping at the eager pussy of her own Mistress, who took a firm grip of her hair too, and played into her appreciation of hair pulling. To have Susanna tugging at her, pulling her face in and demanding that Amber pleasure her, was wonderfully relaxing. Amber felt so comfortable, it felt so right that she should be on her knees, worshipping her Mistress, submitting to her body and soul.

It was truly her rightful place in the world, to be wherever Susanna needed her, to be her pet, her pony, her loyal assistant, her playful slut. The party a few weeks ago, had driven it all home to her, when her Mistress had shared her quite freely with her friends. Being publicly used, teased, punished and fucked had put Amber's feelings of submission into a whole new context for her.

Now, she was to be given over for a week to the control of another domme, who was currently fucking her vigorously with a strap-on cock. Amber was going to be trained in new skills in order to pleasure her own Mistress and be expected to pleasure her trainer and be disciplined by her.

The way that Mistress Chevalier was fucking her, was distinctive from the way Mistress Susanna had. It was more aggressive, rougher and felt more like she was being taken for Mistress Chevalier's pleasure, rather than sensually fucked.

Amber hadn't been nosy enough to find out Mistress Susanna's age, but while she was older, she would guess that her Mistress was in her late thirties, not much more than ten years older than her. Mistress Chevalier on the other hand, was more likely in her fifties, just over twice her age.

Mistress Chevalier wasn't slender and graceful in the way that Susanna was. A cruel person might have called her stout or stocky but she wasn't greatly overweight or truly unfit. In fact, while she was curvaceous, the way she was pounding Amber's pussy gave good evidence of how fit the older woman was.

It was strangely arousing to be used by an older woman who could have been one of her mother's friends or one of her professors. To know that soon Mistress Susanna would leave for London and she would be left entirely at the mercy of Mistress Chevalier. The domme was charged with training her as a ponygirl, which Amber was willing to try if it pleased Mistress Susanna, but was still unsure if she would take to it as Ginger and the others did.

Amber imagined that the training would be reinforced with spanking, caning, floggers and whips. Given the events at the party, Amber had no doubt that Mistress Chevalier would use her sexually, just as much as Mistress Susanna did and that she would enjoy every second of that. Even the corporal punishment she would be subjected to would make her aroused, and her pussy wet.

The combination of fucking, the taste and feel of her Mistress's pussy, the fingers in her hair and the thoughts of what the next week would be like, brought her to a rousing climax. Amber found herself moaning loudly into Mistress Susanna's sex as her body shuddered with wave after wave of pleasure.

Mistress Chevalier was relentless, calling her a good girl and complimenting her on coming like the slut she was, but not stopping her thrusting motions for a heartbeat. Amber's pussy was sensitive from her climax but she wasn't allowed any respite.

"You can have a break when you make your Mistress come, slut," Mistress Chevalier said, as if Amber's every shudder, moan and movement, where an open book to her. Amber wondered how many girls she'd fucked like this to be able to read her so easily.

Regardless, Amber dug deep within herself and found a reservoir of untapped talent, revitalising her efforts and forcing herself to concentrate on the increasingly rapid breathing of her Mistress. Anything was better than thinking about the wildly sensitive folds of her pussy which Mistress Chevalier continued to stimulate.

Mistress Chevalier was proved a liar, as she didn't stop when Mistress Susanna had screamed her way through an impressive orgasm. It wasn't until Mistress Susanna finally came back to her senses, and Amber had been cruelly forced to a second orgasm that left her pussy aching and tears in her eyes, that she waved the other domme away.

"Well done, Amber. You handled that fucking quite impressively," Mistress Chevalier said.

"Thank you, Mistress Chevalier," Amber gasped panting.

Mistress Chevalier smacked her bottom hard, making Amber yelp in shock, before she pulled back and the large silicone dildo plopped out of her.

Mistress Susanna smiled down at her, "Amber, clean that off like a good slut."

Mistress Chevalier didn't wait for Amber to turn around, she reached down and grabbed her hair, pulling her roughly into position. Amber was turned around and pushed against the seat next to Mistress Chevalier. Still sitting on the floor, her back arched and her head, just touching the cushion.

Mistress Chevalier crouched, and, still holding Amber's head by the hair, pushed the silicone into her mouth deep enough to come close to choking her, "Suck it, you filthy slut!"

Amber heard her Mistress chuckling as she was forced to suck the dildo and clean it with her tongue, the process leaving her gasping for air and her eyes watering.

When Mistress Chevalier was satisfied and backed off, Amber collapsed back against the firm cushion behind her, turning her head to look up at Mistress Susanna. Her domme had an almost demonic look of lust on her face and the fingers idly strumming her clit, bore witness to how much she'd enjoyed watching Amber subjugated by her friend.

Mistress Susanna reached out her spare hand and stroked the back of Amber's head, as she licked her lips in a manner that Amber could only see as predatory.

"Thank you for a lovely day, Jade," Mistress Susanna said.

"No, thank you, and your wonderful slut. I'm looking forward to training her for you. I do hope you enjoy the results."

"I'm sure I will, but this is my last night at the house for a while, so I think I'm going to take Amber back to my room and ravish her to say goodbye," Mistress Susanna replied.

"I think that's a good idea. I should probably spend some time with Vicky before she starts pinning anyway," Mistress Chevalier said, absent-mindedly stroking the length of silicone which still hung between her legs.

"From tomorrow, you'll have complete access to Amber to help you keep Vicky happy," Mistress Susanna replied. "You'll like that, won't you, Amber?"

"Yes, Mistress."

CHAPTER 6

"Now, Amber, I'm going to ask you some questions so that you can demonstrate that you understand the standard signals. One stamp for yes, two stamps for no, three if you need to use your safeword," Mistress Chevalier said. "Understood?"

Amber stomped her foot, not too hard, just firmly enough for a clear clopping sound to ring out across the concrete of the yard. It wasn't quite like the sound of a real pony's hoof, but it was close enough for roleplaying. The thick rod of rubber that was clenched between her back teeth left her unable to speak clearly.

"Good girl," Mistress Chevalier said. "Would you like me to give you a dozen hard strokes of the cane?"

Two stamps answered that question.

"Very well. Are you sure?"

Amber stamped once.

Mistress Chevalier reached out, stroking the back of her fingers against Amber's cheek. It was the lightest of touches, just barely enough for Amber to feel the line the older woman was tracing. Her temporary Mistress turned her hand over, running the very tips of her fingers down Amber's neck, skipping lightly over the leather straps of her harness, and ghosting over the swell of her breast.

Amber shivered in anticipation, the hairs on the back of her neck standing up. She had been ordered to stand up straight, shoulders back and keep her breasts pushed forward to display herself well for her trainer. *Would Mistress touch her more intimately, Amber wondered?*

"You have such soft, beautiful skin, Amber," Mistress whispered, "do you moisturise?"

One stamp.

"This nipple," Mistress started as her finger traced a wide circle around the compact areola that cover the tip of Amber's left breast, "seems stiff. Swollen. Firm. Would you like me to touch it?"

One stamp. The gentle fingers alighted on the puckered flesh, with the merest hint of pressure. "You like that, don't you, being teased? Does my ponygirl like being teased?"

Amber clomped her foot again, her voice breaking into her first attempt at a whinny.

"Oh, my! That is simply adorable, Vicky. Did you hear, Amber gave her first whinny."

Of course, Vicky was also dressed in character as a ponygirl, so she too gave a foot stomp and an encouraging whinny.

"Amber, I am tempted to lick and suck and tease these nipples of yours, until you are quite wet," Mistress Chevalier suggested. "Would you enjoy that?" she asked, receiving a single stomp and a look that implored her to act. Mistress Chevalier gave a somewhat filthy laugh at that.

"I would far rather take each of your beautiful nubbins between my thumb and forefinger, and pinch them hard, twisting them until tears come to your eyes, though. Does that also meet with your approval?" Mistress Chevalier asked, as she moved to stand directly in front of Amber, both hands now tantalisingly fluttering over the submissive's breasts and erect nipples.

Amber stomped her foot twice, vigorously rejecting the idea.

"No? You don't want me to use your nipples to bring you pain?" Mistress Chevalier said, her heavily overacted shock, entirely feigned. Amber stamped her foot twice once more.

"You really don't, do you?" Mistress Chevalier said, with a pout and a flutter of her eyelashes. "If I do it anyway, because it pleases me to hurt you, will you let me do it, anyway?"

Amber swallowed, nodding as she stomped her foot once.

"Even though you don't want to feel such pain?"

Another affirmative.

"Will it make that sweet quim of yours, flood with arousal? Amber, will it make you wet?" Mistress Chevalier asked.

Amber knew that it would, knew that the pain that was coming would be more than she could bear to receive, less just enough for Mistress Chevalier to retain control of her body and mind. Enough to make Amber's tears run freely with tears and a whisker less than would have her ending play by using her safeword.

There was no doubt in her mind, that with all Mistress Chevalier's years of experience, she had played this sort of game to perfection many times. The pain she would experience would balance on the knife edge of her limit and leave her on the verge of what she still saw as defeat.

Mistress Susanna had counselled her that the safeword was neither to be used lightly, for that would spoil the fun of both Mistress and submissive, nor was it to be avoided at all costs, risking physical harm or mental anguish to the sub.

Amber swallowed, took a deep breath, and stomped her foot once.

Mistress Chevalier gave her a peck on the cheek, then her fingers tightened like hot vices on Amber's nipples, cruelly tugging and twisting at them. Amber's eyes did indeed fill with tears, she stomped her foot twice, but struggled against the impulse to put it down a third time.

The older woman's eyes were alive with sadistic glee as Amber's gagged mouth gurgled out half a scream of pain at the rough treatment.

When Amber sucked in a breath to begin screaming again, as cumbersome as it was around the bit gag in her mouth, Mistress Chevalier dipped her right hand between Amber's creamy thighs. Her fingers found the submissive's lips, quickly parting them and rubbing at her aching clit roughly. Amber was positively gushing, her arousal far beyond the ability to deny it.

Two fingers, wet with Amber's juices were slid between her lips, under the bar of the gag, allowing her to taste her own sex.

Then the sharp pain in her nipples again, as Mistress Chevalier, with a cruel laugh, twisted them in the reverse direction. This fresh version elicited the arousal response, but the pain felt somehow different, perhaps because Amber's nipples were already bruised or perhaps it was psychological.

Whatever the cause, Amber began to weep softly, actual tears dripping down her cheeks, even as trails of liquid streaked the inside of her thighs and betrayed her pleasure.

"How beautiful you are, Amber. It's a delight to enjoy your suffering," Mistress Chevalier complimented her.

When the bit was unbuckled from one side of her face, Amber thought she might be granted leave to speak, something which Mistress Chevalier had said was strictly forbidden for an in character ponygirl. Stomps of the foot, head shakes, whinnying and neighing, were all permitted. Only human speech and sounds were restricted.

If the feet or legs were restrained, bound or in use in a way that prevented the expression of yes, no or the safeword through stomps, slaps against the leg with the palm of the hand would be used.

It was not to permit speech that the pressure on her cheeks was relieved, it was to permit Mistress Chevalier to access and possess Amber's mouth with her hot tongue. Amber found herself in a hungry kiss, being taken and used by her trainer, her mouth dominated by the questing muscle. It did nothing to reduce her level of arousal of course, it merely heightened it.

Not that Amber would have objected to such a passionate kiss, in any case. Her nipples were sore, even as Mistress more gently fondled her breasts while they kissed, but the kiss itself was divine and Amber lost herself to it for as long as Mistress Chevalier chose to draw it out.

"How delightful you are, Pony Amber," Mistress Chevalier said, looking at her expectantly.

Amber returned the look and took a deep breath. The look on the older woman's face betrayed an expectation and Amber hesitated, before happily whinnying her response.

Mistress Chevalier cracked a half smile at that, proud that her lessons were being absorbed.

"Good pony," she said, offering the flat of her palm.

Amber blushed when she saw the sugar lump treat that was being offered.

The embarrassment at being treated like this, didn't stop her dipping her head and scooping it up with her tongue, of course.

Even human ponies liked sugar cubes.

CHAPTER 7

It took a few hours for Mistress Chevalier to go through the process of putting the ponygirl harness and tack on another girl and then herself. Vicky was Amber's practice partner, which Mistress Chevalier explained in terms of rope bunnies. Amber didn't like to admit that she had no idea what a rope bunny was and made a mental note to look it up later.

At every stage, the importance of a good fit and checking things thoroughly was stressed. The harnesses for pulling a cart were quite different to those that were purely fetish costumes to create an appearance and once she was shown, the padding and attachment points made the separation obvious. A costume harness would break or risk injuring the pony girl if you tried to pull on it and looked less stylish at an indoor party.

The saddles were quite different. Some were intended to be used for a pony on all fours, so their dominant could sit directly on their back, but some were for a pony to be ridden while they were upright. It was like carrying someone on your back with their legs around your waist and your arms under their knees.

Amber didn't think she'd be able to do that at all, and she certainly wouldn't be able to carry Vicky, but they put a saddle on the muscular ponygirl and Amber got to ride her around briefly.

When Mistress Chevalier put Amber on all fours, saddled her and rode her around the tack room, that was relatively easy. Amber didn't have to bear the full weight of another person on her arms and the rider could easily put their feet down.

It was very slow to get about though and easy to see why pulling the traps and chariots was so popular and outdoor play was such a key part of the ponygirls repertoire. Mistress Chevalier explained that playing outdoors had a host of problems, mostly to do with privacy and the weather, but the sheer expense was off-putting too many people.

"You're lucky to have met Susanna so you can try this out in such excellent facilities, Amber. I'm really very grateful that you suggested that she refurbish more of the stables and let me run my workshop here. I think this is going to be a fantastic year," Mistress Chevalier said while they took Vicky's outfit off again so that Amber could give it another go.

"There, all done. Over to you. Do you think you can get it all on, in the correct order, without prompting?" Mistress Chevalier asked. "There's a treat in store for you if you do."

"Yes, Mistress," Amber replied. "I think I have it."

"Very well, I'll only chip in if you are doing anything truly bad. It's a dozen strokes if you miss anything or get it out of sequence. Proceed," Mistress Chevalier instructed.

"Yes, Mistress."

Amber set about getting the harness, bit and bridle, hoof boots and so on, correctly fitted to Vicky, trying hard to make sure she got them on in the correct order that Mistress Chevalier had laid out.

There were some items that were easier to put on first for instance, the bridle could be fitted and the bit put in place later so that the pony could still give verbal responses while you checked the fit.

The last thing that Amber had to fit was the pony tail that all the girls wore some version of. There were quite a few spare ones available, and some novelty options like a rainbow coloured one for unicorns, as well as some other types of tails for piggy play or puppy play. But each girl also had her own labelled butt plugs with tails for pony play.

Vicky's seemed quite large to Amber but wasn't grossly outsized. It was made of shining steel and the tail hair itself was quite realistic, at least, to Amber's far from expert eye.

Fitting the pony girls with their butt plug tails was Amber's favourite part of this process so far. Coating two fingers of her right hand with liberal helpings of lubricant, she instructed Vicky to bend over and assume the position. It would be easy as this wasn't their first time today but Mistress Chevalier had made it clear she was to go through all the stages each time for practice, even though Vicky was used to having toys inserted between her firm buttocks.

Amber gently probed Vicky's welcoming ring of muscle, as if it weren't already prepared and quite well lubricated. She teased the rosebud of flesh, listening for Vicky's reaction, every gasp and murmur as she slowly worked a finger knuckle deep into the body-builder.

"Good girl, Vicky," Amber said, "can you take more?"

Vicky stomped one foot, though her bit was free at this point and Amber grinned, licking her lips as she leaned down to see what she was doing in detail. She watched as Vicky's tight, glistening ring of flesh comfortably swallowed her second finger. The ponygirl gasped with pleasure as Amber began to thrust her fingers slowly in and out of her.

Not wanting to get the dozen strokes though, Amber couldn't push her luck and soon had to lubricate the butt plug with a light coating of liquid and slowly fill the space her fingers had vacated with it. She wiped her fingers on some antibacterial wipes and dried her hands on a towel, before putting Vicky's bit gag in place and checking all the straps for a final time.

"I think this is correct, Mistress," Amber said, trying to sound calm.

Mistress Chevalier nodded, "Very well, take a seat while I inspect your work."

The older woman ran her finger under straps that needed to have some give and tugged gently at the points where a cart would be attached to check everything was properly fitted. She pressed and tugged at the butt plug as well, but Amber got the impression part of her motivation for that was to torment her ponygirl, Vicky, not just check Amber's work.

Finally Mistress Chevalier pronounced the work to be good and congratulated Amber on a job well done.

"I think it's time you have a reward for your hard work and concentration, don't you, Amber?"

"Thank you, Mistress," Amber said.

"Get Vicky out of that harness, and then both of you can join me in our lovely new flat," Mistress Chevalier ordered.

"Yes, Mistress," Amber said for them both, as Vicky was still gagged.

CHAPTER 8

Mistress Chevalier was quite naked when the girls had put away the ponygirl gear and was reclining on the four poster bed that she had brought to the flat with her. A long rattan school cane lay ominously on the mattress beside her and she smiled as the two submissives, so very different in appearance, entered the bedroom.

"Amber, help Vicky put on that strap-on, there's a dear," she ordered with a wicked gleam in her eyes.

At the foot of the bed, a purple leather harness and dildo lay waiting for them. Amber knelt before Vicky and held the harness open for her to step into, Jiggling it up her thighs and slowly tightening and adjusting the straps until the fit was secure but so tight it would be uncomfortable.

The dildo itself was also purple, to match the colour of the harness and it didn't get any more realistic when it came to the shape of the thing either. It had a bit of a curve to it, small nodules along the length in a spiral pattern around it, and it was if it was a series of balls squashed together, rather than a rod. It would open someone wider, let them close, then open them up again, as you thrust it home, rather like anal beads.

The head of the thing was a comically proportioned mushroom head, with a rounded tip and an exaggerated flair around the base. Amber wondered how Mistress Chevalier took such an intrusion, as the head of the dildo widened at its base, protruding like the brim of a big, purple hat. Pushing that through any opening would force it wide, before it was inside and the entrance could close around the thick shaft.

Amber had seen much larger toys, although not in use but this one would force the recipient to open and close as each new ball was slid into them. A part of her wondered if Mistress Chevalier had ever used it on some poor girls bottom, or if it was only used for more usual intercourse.

Vicky gave her hips an experimental jiggle left and right, and then a few thrusts which came perilously close to Amber's face. She flinched back, not wanting to get a black eye from the monstrous purple silicone cock.

"Amber, you may get up here now and please me with your tongue. On all fours so that Vicky can fuck your sweet pussy with her toy," Mistress Chevalier said, with a casual tone that didn't seem to suit the immensity of the words. When Amber had seen the harness and dildo, she had imagined, perhaps naively, that she would not be the one receiving it.

Taking her time, Amber slowly got on the bed, and crawled forward, kissing Mistress Chevalier's calves, her knees, and her inner thighs as she advanced on her. She was playing for time, trying to get the picture of the enormous tool out of her mind.

When the mattress sunk behind her legs at the additional weight of Vicky kneeling on it, Amber knew she didn't have much longer before she would be impaled on the thing. Refusing to be subjected to it was an option, and a request for something smaller might be received well. Knowing, intellectually, that her anatomy was capable of taking larger things, didn't mean she wanted to find out what giving birth was like in reverse.

Amber smiled, teasing Mistress Chevalier, edging slowly forward, as the domme rolled her hips invitingly, waiting for the young submissive to apply her tongue where it was needed.

"Come to me, pet, stop teasing and show me what you've learned," Mistress Chevalier growled lustily, beckoning to Amber.

Steeling herself for what was to come, Amber finally moved forward, and dipped her head between the dominant woman's thighs, her tongue soon questing for its target in the curved join between Mistress Chevalier's lips.

"Yes, that's where you are best employed, you saucy wench. Just like that," Mistress Chevalier encouraged. The domme's hands stroked and squeezed her own breasts, playing with her nipples as Amber began to suck and lick at her lips and clit.

For a few delicious moments, Amber forgot about her impending appointment with Vicky's strap-on. Then the time was upon her and she had to struggle to keep the reasoning side of her mind in action, concentrating on pleasuring Mistress Chevalier rather than what was going on behind her.

A bottle of lubricant made an obscene spurting noise as it was aimed directly at her lower back. The cool liquid pooled in the small of her back and Vicky dipped her fingers in, using Amber's curves as a palette to work from. Amber could hear the slippery fluid squelching as Vicky rubbed her hand up and down the dildo giving it a thorough covering.

Then Vicky's big, gym fit fingers slapped a big dollop against Amber's already wet pussy, smearing the cold fluid all over her, before she began to work first one, then two fingers inside. Amber squirmed in anticipation. Extra lubrication wasn't something she usually needed, after all she was still only in her early to mid-twenties and it wasn't as if the humiliating, wicked and sometimes painful games she'd been subjected to since joining Mistress Susanna's household, didn't turn her on. In fact, she'd never been so regularly and thoroughly turned on, even as a horny first-year student, since Susanna had introduced her to Sapphic pleasures.

No, Amber didn't normally require additional lubrication, unless her bottom was the target and her arsehole needed to admit fingers or a butt plug. This wasn't the first time Vicky had played with her, so if she was adding lube she must expect it was needed. That toy had seemed big, but perhaps Vicky's huge frame made it seem smaller than it was. She must be expecting Amber to struggle with additional help. Just how big was it, really? Or was it partly the undulating bulbs that required the extra lube so that Vicky could fuck her rapidly and roughly, with the whole length of the exotically designed shaft.

Vicky didn't stop at thrusting 3 fingers into Amber's pussy to open her up, she added a fourth and used them like a spike to widen the young submissive's hungry pussy. Each powerful stroke forward distended Amber in a way that approached being uncomfortable, while feeling utterly filthy and desirable at the same time. Vicky's hands were on the large side, but she nevertheless kept going until Amber was so opened up, that her lips stretched out to admit Vicky's hand past the third knuckle.

Amber fairly howled into Mistress Chevalier's pussy as Vicky drove her wild with lust as her hand was swallowed to the wrist. Vicky grunted in surprise, "I didn't think she was going to take it all, but the greedy little harlot practically swallowed me when I gave her enough to think about it. Look, Mistress, she's got my whole hand in her."

"She has, hasn't she," Mistress Chevalier agreed. "What a greedy little slut you are, Amber? Vicky has such big hands and you're taking her fist like a champion filly, aren't you?"

Amber's tongue was still lapping at Mistress Chevalier's lips as she strove to remain focused but with Vicky's whole hand buried in her cunt it was almost impossible.

Mistress Chevalier took a firm grip on her head with both hands and tilted her face up so she could look down her body into Amber's eyes. "Is that what you are, Amber? A greedy little slut who loves to be filled up and fucked hard?"

Amber gasped as Vicky's hand withdrew, perfectly timed with the demand from their dominant, her big knuckles opening her to her widest as they were dragged out past her soaking entrance and her pussy contracted as the width of the intrusion lessened.

"Yes, Mistress!" she yelped. "I'm a filthy whore and I love being filled up with Vicky's hand."

"Do you like being fisted by Vicky?"

"I love it, Mistress. I love having her big hand buried in my pussy."

"You are such a bad girl, Amber," Mistress Chevalier said, picking up the cane with a menacing look. Amber groaned as Vicky's hand pushed in past the knuckles again.

Her eyes were still locked to Mistress Chevalier's who tutted as Amber groaned her pleasure at being fisted. With a scowl that could have been genuine or expert roleplaying for all Amber could tell in her current state, she brought the cane whistling down across Amber's buttocks with a crack that filled the room.

Amber screamed and cursed, calling Mistress Chevalier a rude name that she felt sure would anger the domme and result in more severe chastisement.

Mistress Chevalier was far from upset, the vulgarity seemed to inflame her passion if anything. She became more exuberant, as she striped Amber's bottom. "Yes, let it all out, Amber. Curse at me all you want while I punish you for being a filthy slut," the domme laughed, counting each stroke out as she delivered a dozen hard whacks, even as Amber reached a massive climax.

Amber's body shuddered as Vicky's fist pumped back and forth throughout her orgasm, and their domme continued to thrash her with the cane. It was only when she stopped shaking from her climax that Mistress Chevalier ordered Vicky to pull out, which she did to the accompaniment of a wet sound.

"Excellent. Vicky, fuck her now, while Amber puts her sweet mouth back to work for me," Mistress ordered as she grabbed Amber's head and pushed it back down to her waiting lips.

Vicky wasted no time in positioning the big, undulating cock and impaling Amber with it. It was done with skill but with no finesse or subtlety. The strap-on replaced the big woman's hand and slid inside her, without opposition. Vicky was an expert with the toy and soon built up a fast paced rhythm that set Amber on a path straight back up the peak she had only just descended.

"Keep going Vicky, Amber is loving every minute of you fucking her, aren't you slut?" Mistress Chevalier asked. Amber mumbled into the delicious meal she was consuming but wasn't allowed a breath to respond audibly so she lifted one hand and gave a big thumbs up signal. That drew a chuckle from Mistress Chevalier and a noticeable tightening of the grip on Amber's hair.

"As you command, Mistress," Vicky rumbled, not sounding like she was unhappy in the slightest. Judging by the way she alternately slapped Amber's sore bottom and gripped her hips tightly to fuck her even harder, Vicky was thoroughly enjoying herself.

Amber wondered if Vicky was really a submissive at all, or just a filthy bitch who loved to fuck women and be fucked. If she could have spoken, she might very well have asked the same question, in just as rude a manner, and been duly punished for her vulgarity. Amber knew that that prospect would only encourage her to be rude though, not put her off.

"The little trollop is coming, Mistress," Vicky said, as if this was a terrible infringement of the rules somehow, although it did not go unnoticed by Amber that the big woman didn't slow her pace or cease slapping and fondling her sensitive bum cheeks.

"You're not to come without my permission, Amber. That's very naughty of you. You'll have to make Vicky come twice with your tongue now, as punishment. And me three times," Mistress Chevalier warned. The domme pulled Amber's head up so she could speak, "What do you say to that, my girl?"

"Yes, Mistress."

CHAPTER 9

"No, no, no! Knees up higher!" Mistress Chevalier ordered.

Amber was parading around the yard, performing steps for her domme like an army recruit being shouted at by her drill instructor. Of course, when the army broke down a raw recruit, the seemingly harsh treatment was to ensure they could take orders in battle.

A ponygirl had no such life-saving motivation. Amber's reason for doing all this was to try this out for her beloved Mistress Susanna and discover if a life of sexual roleplaying as a human pony appealed to her. If she had as much of a thing for it as Pepper or Ginger, she might be offered a new role instead of being Susanna's personal assistant.

The addition of a colleague walking behind her with a riding crop, and delivering three firm swats with it when she made an error, was another deviation from the way the armed forces did things. Vicky wasn't sparing the rod either, each blow caused Amber to whimper around the bit gag in her mouth. Mistress Chevalier had ordered her not to try to run away or dodge Vicky's inducements, or else she'd let the big ponygirl chase her down and invent her own punishments.

Amber had already determined that Vicky was a filthy pervert who delighted in making the other submissives suffer. Any chance to inflict corporal punishment on the other girls was taken without hesitation or guilt. Her sadism and cruelty were different to that of Mistress Chevalier or Mistress Susanna as well. Vicky didn't hold back because she was a submissive herself, not even a little.

"Stop. Give me six jumping jacks," Mistress Chevalier ordered. The training sessions weren't just about her physical form and ability to follow instructions, Amber's temporary domme liked to include plenty of calisthenic exercise as well. The domme claimed this was to ensure the ponygirls were fit and healthy and could perform their duties.

Amber rather thought it was also because she enjoyed their humiliation as their bare breasts bounced up and down in the harnesses which surrounded and accentuated them, but offered nothing in the way of support. None of Mistress Susanna's girl had anything to be ashamed of in the health or looks department, they were all in fairly good shape, well-groomed and naturally pretty. But it wasn't about looks, so much as the feeling they were not meeting some standard or the pressure they felt to be normal girls. Modest girls. Chaste girls.

There was no real room for modesty and certainly not chastity, on Mistress Susanna's estate, but the feeling that she should not be nude, being paraded for the pleasure of other women, or publicly flogged and caned, felt real all the same. Only it didn't make Amber want to give in. It just made her more aroused, knowing there was something somehow naughty about what they were doing. Submitting to the hedonistic pleasures of the older women who held sway on the estate from day to day, or during Mistress's infrequent parties, was humbling but also thrilling.

The sense of mortification was accompanied by a bravado that made Amber feel like quite the exhibitionist, even though everyone who could see her without a telescope or satellite, was in on the events. Being watched by all those lascivious women at the party had been a complete thrill.

After the jumping jacks it was press-ups and then jogging on the spot until Amber thought her legs would turn to rubbery stalks and collapse under her.

Eventually, she was sent back to the tack room at a gallop, with

Vicky chasing after her, swatting her across the buttocks with her crop every time she caught up. Amber went as fast as she could, and Vicky could clearly have outpaced her but held back. There was just enough crop to keep Amber motivated and heated, and not so much that she completely lost balance.

Amber had only a few moments of breathing space to calm down before Mistress Chevalier had strode across the yard from the fence she usually perched on while instructing the girls, and joined them in the tack room. The domme took up a seat on a thickly padded bench and clicked her fingers, indicating that Amber should approach.

"Turn away from me. Good, now straddle my legs and sit down," Mistress Chevalier ordered. Amber did as she was told, still in her harness. The bit and bridle were removed, and Vicky was told to take off the hoof boots as well. Amber could have got them off but having help was so much quicker. She wiggled her toes as they were freed from the demanding footwear.

Mistress Chevalier parted her knees and took a firm grip on Amber's upper thighs, "Lean forward until your palms are on the floor."

Although Amber wasn't a gymnast by any means, she was able to perform the manoeuvre without help from Vicky, which was comforting and less embarrassing than having to ask for assistance from the giantess. The dominant woman repositioned her until she was satisfied and then dipped her head.

Upside down and face flushed with blood, Amber was surprised when the agile tongue of the Stable Mistress, delved between her lips and sought out her engorged nubbin. Mistress Chevalier was even better at eating pussy than Sugar or Candy, whose cunnilingus skills were considered the most expert of the women who lived on the estate.

Years of practice, serving older dominant women at first, and later as a dominant lesbian herself, had taught Mistress Chevalier every trick in the book. Despite being dominant, she had no hesitation about using her tongue to pleasure her submissives.

A part of Amber's mind was surprised that the outwardly entirely dominant woman should be happy to eat pussy, because it seemed like it should be a submissive act. Another part said the pussy belonged to Mistress Chevalier, and she could eat it, fuck it, or torment it as she chose.

It was the second part that won out, because it was so very, very delightful to have her cunt worshipped by an avoid connoisseur of the art form. Amber had rapidly grown accustomed to performing cunnilingus on whom ever Mistress Susanna ordered and had developed quite the taste for it, she thought. Her enjoyment was nothing quite like the gusto with which Mistress Chevalier faced the challenge though.

To delay her own orgasm, which Amber knew was rising fast, she concentrated on identifying the motions and techniques Mistress Chevalier was using against her wet lips and clit. Trying to evaluate them and memorise them, but being upside down was making it hard to concentrate, not to mention the rising tide of pleasure which threatened to flood the play zone any moment.

"Come for me, slut," Mistress Chevalier ordered. The degrading terms that the dominant women frequently used for Amber, might once have offended her, but now she savoured the coarse, humiliating language. The demeaning language simply aroused her, and she took pride in being a slut, a trollop, a whore or a filthy little bitch.

Amber was in service to a great woman, who looked after her and brought her both pleasure and pain, beyond her wildest fantasies. If being subjected to words, some might find dehumanising was part of the game, Amber wasn't going to stop playing.

It wasn't long before she had an explosive orgasm, as ordered. Mistress Chevalier's greedy tongue plunged between her moist lips as if she was in a frenzy to consume every ounce of her submissive's pussy. Pursed around Amber's clit, the lips allowed the domme to apply strong suction as the tip of her tongue teased the nubbin.

There was no hope of resisting the rising wave of her orgasm and Amber screamed in delight as she came hard. Her dominant did not stop licking and sucking at her sensitive slickness until Amber's thighs stopped trembling. Then she was indelicately flipped up the right way, her eyes swimming as her head rushed with the roar of shifting blood.

"Explain why I did that, Amber," Mistress Chevalier ordered, licking her lips free of her submissive's juices as she waited for an answer.

Amber swallowed hard while she formulated her answer as quickly as she could. "You did it because you reward ponygirls who are good and punish ponygirls who are bad, Mistress."

"And how do I punish bad ponygirls, Amber?"

"You enjoy all sorts of punishments and discipline, Mistress but I think you favour the cane."

"Correct. Now, on your knees girl, I want your tongue on my clit while Vicky cane's your beautifully pert bottom until you make me come twice," Mistress Chevalier said, leaning back on the bench as Amber dismounted and got to her knees at the end of it.

"Begin," Mistress Chevalier ordered as Amber's head dipped between her legs.

Vicky's cane landed the first blow even as Amber's lips emulated her Mistress's technique and pursed around the dominant woman's clit so she could suck on it and run the tip of her tongue across it.

"Make that three times, Amber," Mistress Chevalier said with a yelp as Amber's wicked tongue really got to work. "Make me come three times, and Vicky will stop caning you."

"Yes, Mistress."

CHAPTER 10

The following morning Amber spent the whole time learning how to pull a larger trap than she'd used for racing. It was really more of an open topped carriage than a trap, with four wheels and enough space for several passengers. Mistress Chevalier was the only one today, and Vicky, Ginger and Pepper were pulling alongside Amber.

It looked quite similar to the racing traps that Mistress Susanna owned, and the ones that Mistress Chevalier had brought with her, at least in the style of components and manufacturing. The carriage was built to be as light as possible but with just a few more creature comforts for the passengers.

Being harnessed to the carriage was also quite different, as the girls were in two pairs side by side like real horses pulling a coach. Pulling and handling the carriage involved the same commands for turning, stopping and accelerating, and required the same responses to the reins but Amber had to learn to work with the team.

It was important that the ponygirls work together and not pull against each other or move too fast or too slowly, lest they cause an accident. If they didn't pull together someone would end up stumbling, and they'd have to stop. If they went too fast, again, someone would stumble or wear themselves out and stopping was a team effort too.

Mistress Chevalier explained that the lightweight of the carriage was more about being able to stop it easily, than the girls ability to pull it. Since bodybuilders could pull huge delivery trucks on their own, there was ample proof that the weight wasn't much of an issue in getting going. Since they wanted to travel at a faster than walking pace though, lightweight construction let them accelerate more easily and meant they could slow down safely too.

There was an unexpected benefit to the girls that Amber welcomed - the inability for the driver to whip them all. The two lead ponies were protected by the two rear ponies, so any whipping was restricted to their unfortunate buttocks. But Mistress Chevalier cracked the whip above their heads instead of applying lashes to their bodies and that gave them the emphatic guidance they needed, just as well as a stripe across their bottom would.

At the end of the morning, Amber and the team had got a good rhythm going and Mistress Chevalier took them out for a lap of the lake, driving them progressively faster as they rounded the end and started on the home stretch.

By the time the ponygirls drew to a stop in the yard outside the stables, all four were drenched in sweat and breathing hard, gulping in big lungful's of air. Amber would have sworn she could hear her heart pounding in her chest and the rush of blood in her ears.

No time was wasted on their recovery though. Mistress Chevalier had them walk the carriage close to the coach house set aside for storing the various conveyances the ponygirls pulled and then began getting them out of their harness. Amber was freed first so that she could release Vicky behind her, then they pulled and pushed the carriage into the coach house and shut it up.

After that, Mistress Chevalier took them to the tack room, where they stripped each other of their harness and cleaned everything off properly. They used anti-bacterial toy wipes for the butt plugs which supported their tails. Each toy and bit of leather was cleaned appropriately, inspected for damage or wear and returned to its allocated storage space.

"Off to the showers!" Mistress Chevalier barked when they were all done, marching them to the changing area which was dominated by a large, white-tiled shower space with a dozen or so shower heads fixed to the wall. There were a few cubicles, but those were reserved for the dominants, while the open shower area was for the submissives.

They were already naked as they filed into the shower room under the stern gaze of the Stable Mistress. Amber saw that Mistress Chevalier was holding the garden hose with the spray attachment and her shoulders slumped. That meant cold water first.

"Line up, face the wall," Mistress Chevalier said, flicking the trigger on the spray and spattering them with cold water, making them all squeal in shock.

Once they were lined up, Mistress Chevalier went after each of them in turn, soaking them thoroughly and getting the mud and sweat of their backs. Then they turned around, screwed their eyes shut and were given the same treatment again.

Amber knew this wasn't about cleanliness, this was about the older woman enjoying seeing the girls reactions as the cold water covered their skin in goose-bumps and turned their nipples to stiff nubs. Mistress Chevalier had done this to them before, only letting them shower with soap after she'd had her sadistic fun with them and the hose.

"Turn around and bend over, feet shoulder width apart," Mistress Chevalier ordered.

This was new, thought Amber. Mistress Chevalier had stopped by now, on the days where she'd used this particular torment.

"Put your hands behind you, grasp your cheeks firmly and pull them apart. Make sure I can see everything you sluts have on offer," their domme ordered.

Amber did as she was told, feeling butterflies of anticipation inside her as she exposed her puckered hole and the lips of her sex to the older woman's lingering glances. She felt her cheeks flush red as a blush rose from her neck up to her ears. Mistress Chevalier could surely see how aroused she was by the state of her lips which were not just wet because of the hose. She wondered how the other girls looked. Were they equally aroused? It was almost a given, and she surely wasn't any more of a slut than any of them.

Then came the hose. Icy water set to a thin high pressure jet smacked against Amber's bottom and she yelped. The spray was powerful and she could feel it dimpling her flesh as it was played across each bottom in turn a few times, before coming back to be directed at the top of Amber's cleft.

The water hammered against her sensitive skin as it probed her tight ring of muscle, like an undulating finger, then down over her lips. Amber whimpered as her most intimate parts were cooled right down. It was truly perverted to be used like this, aroused by the attentions of an older woman and then cooled off so mechanically.

Had the water been warm, Amber had no doubt she could have come from the way it pounded on her arsehole and pussy alone. But the water was not warm, and that was quite deliberate. There was a mixer tap in the room that the hose could be attached to that would provide hot or warm water quite readily but Mistress Chevalier always used the one on the outside wall of the stables which only provided cold water.

It was her sadistic side that led to such torments, and it wasn't necessary for the ponygirls to come from this game, in order for Mistress Chevalier to receive pleasure. Amber heard each girl give voice to her frustration and the impact of the cold water as their domme tormented their tight bum holes and aching pussies with the water.

Finally the water was switched off, and Mistress Chevalier gave her next instruction. "Pair up and get each other lathered up head to toe, I want you so clean you sparkle."

Amber was claimed by Vicky who pulled her to one of the soap dispensers mounted on the shower wall and put wastefully large handfuls of lemon scented shower gel all over her chest and shoulders. Then the big woman set to work on Amber's cold flesh, rubbing the shower gel all over her to build up a lather and then working at each nook and cranny with methodical attention to detail.

Vicky pinched and rolled Amber's nipples between thumb and forefinger, rubbed at her pussy and slipped fingers inside her covered with the strong citrus gel as well as between her cheeks. When she was done, not an inch of Amber's body remained untouched, though her face had been washed down with a flannel wash cloth and rinsed off immediately to avoid getting soap in her eyes. That was considerate of Vicky who had a sadistic streak that Amber found terrifying and delightful in equal measure, which was borne out by a second round of attention to her breasts once her face was clean. Vicky didn't spend long but her powerful fingers inflicted pressure that had Amber's eyes welling up with tears.

Amber was able to return the favour, starting with the big woman's strong calves and thighs, before burying three soapy fingers in her cunt as she looked up Vicky's body to hold her gaze. The Amazonian looked a little cross but felt aroused as Amber rapidly frigged her, before moving around behind her to work on her powerful buttocks.

Again, Amber used her soapy fingers to penetrate, hearing a grunt of lust from Vicky but no protest from Mistress Chevalier who was leaning against the half-height wall which enclosed the shower space, watching with evident glee. Amber had two fingers in Vicky's arsehole and dripped more soap onto them to ensure she was thoroughly cleaned. Vicky ground back on her intruding digits in a way that suggested she was a little angry with her but badly wanted such treatment all the same. Amber chuckled as she withdrew her fingers and lathered up the rest of Vicky's body.

Having delved so deep in both Vicky's holes, she had to use the secondary shower head on a hose to rinse her out front and back, requiring more penetration to ensure the soap was gone. Vicky growled and gasped as she cleaned her but didn't complain with intelligible words.

"Vicky, Ginger, lean up against the wall. Pepper and Amber, get on your knees and lick their pussies until they cover your pretty faces in their cum," Mistress Chevalier ordered.

Amber and Pepper did as they were told, with excited looks on their faces, worshipping their assigned submissives with all their skill. Given the treatment they'd been having, Amber wasn't surprised when Vicky and Ginger easily reached their peaks and she got her reward of tasting Vicky's orgasm as her juice splashed over Amber's face. A few minutes later they were rinsed off and waiting patiently as Mistress Chevalier removed her thigh length leather boots and stripped off her jodhpurs and blouse before joining them.

Together the four ponygirls worshipfully soaped and rinsed Mistress Chevalier down. The domme took hold of Vicky and Ginger by their heads and guided their mouths to her stiff nipples so they could suckle at her. Looking down at Amber and Pepper she asked, "Pussy or arse, Amber?"

Amber swallowed. "I haven't had the pleasure of worshipping Mistress Susanna's arse yet, Mistress Chevalier," she pointed out.

Mistress Chevalier grunted, "I won't deny her your first time then, so put your tongue between my lips and do a good job, or it's the carpet beater for you, my girl."

Pepper seemed positively thrilled to be the one left with the task of burying her tongue in Mistress Chevalier recently cleaned arsehole. Amber shuddered at the indecency of such an act, finding it quite off-putting. At the same time, she struggled with the thrill it gave her to hear Peppers sloppy noises of delight as she tongued at Mistress Chevalier, rimming her for all she was worth. It was a massive turn on.

"You may all touch yourselves while you pleasure," Mistress Chevalier generously said before warning them, "but do not dare come before I do!"

Amber slipped fingers inside herself, even as she used her other hand to penetrate Mistress Chevalier's defences as her tongue and lips worked magic on the dominant woman's clit.

With four tongues and Amber's fingers working on her at once,

Mistress Chevalier came twice before she decided to take a moment to catch her breath.

The ponygirls quickly washed her down under orders and then lovingly dried their Mistress with large fluffy towels, before they retired for a late lunch.

Mistress Chevalier gathered them all around the table for fresh baguettes and brie, followed by high quality yoghurts as a treat.

Amber's first course was not bread and cheese, but the honour of pleasuring Mistress Chevalier again, kneeling under the table and licking her pussy to another orgasm as the domme chatted calmly to the other ponygirls.

"Good girl, that was a lovely accompaniment to my lunch. You may get up now, and eat your meal," Mistress Chevalier said.

"Yes, Mistress."

CHAPTER 11

"Come, join us in bed, Amber," Mistress Chevalier offered, pointing at the open space between her and her personal submissive, Vicky.

"Should I put my harness on, Mistress?" Amber asked, slightly puzzled as she was currently just wearing a babydoll nightdress she'd been told to put on for the evening meal.

The afternoon had been spent assembling some gym equipment that Mistress Susanna had had delivered, and then being instructed how to use it by the resident expert, Vicky.

All the while, Mistress Chevalier looked on, relaxing on a chaise longue they'd brought in for her to use while they put the new gym together.

Each time Vicky showed the first girl how to use a particular machine, that girl had been summoned, and put to work between Mistress Chevalier's legs. She had told them about the new regimen that would arise from the installation of the gym as well.

"You'll get used to this on a daily basis girls. Mistress Susanna agreed with me that you should all be much fitter than you are and Vicky is going to take charge of your exercise, as Pudding tries to control your diet to keep you healthy. Any girl found shirking her exercise plan will receive personal attention from Vicky and by attention, I mean severe punishment of her choosing, do I make myself clear?"

"Yes, Mistress," the girls had all chorused, although Vicky had been smirking at the other girls with obvious glee at the prospect of punishing them.

Vicky had used powerful pinches and twists of their nipples to emphasise how much faster they should cycle during their cardio routines and Amber's sensitive breasts still ached quite delightfully as a result. Each movement of the sheer negligee against her erect nipples brought both pleasure and pain and her pussy remained wet enough to leave trails of her juices down her inner thighs.

After exercise and a shower was, thankfully, conducted without the accompaniment of a hose, they had all put on various types of nightdress and had a light evening meal together, of salad followed by various fruits.

Mistress Chevalier had played with Pepper at the head of the table, sitting the girl on the table in front of her, and running grapes down the length of her slit before eating them. The other ponygirls had looked on enviously as their domme buried her face in Pepper's sex and brought her to one explosive orgasm after another. Ginger had been allowed to sit on her flatmates mouth, covering it with her sex because of all the noise she was making, after her second orgasm.

Vicky and Amber meanwhile, had been ordered to watch and not touch themselves which had left both of them unutterably horny.

Mistress Chevalier had them all retire to the living room to watch a documentary on ancient lesbian sex cults, which Amber wasn't sure was based on much historical evidence, before announcing it was bedtime.

Now Amber was about to join the older lesbian couple in their bed. Pepper and Ginger had been sent to their own flat with orders to sixty-nine each other until, "your jaws ache and you can't go on", as Mistress Chevalier had put it. Neither had seemed upset by the command, Amber recalled.

"No, I don't need you in harness, Amber. Just take off that babydoll and come and lie down between us," Mistress Chevalier said kindly.

Amber carefully placed the expensive sheer material over the back of a chair and crawled up the bed to lie between the two women. One small and powerful in ways that belied her outward appearance, the other as large and muscular as any woman Amber had ever met with her own power on obvious display in the form of strong thighs and biceps.

Immediately, Vicky pressed her stiff nipples into Amber's back, her leg curling over Amber's and her foot slipping between the smaller woman's calves. With a simple twist of her left leg, Vicky prised Amber's legs apart, trapping Amber's left leg with hers, like a wrestling champion.

"Mistress," Amber began as Vicky's mouth descended possessively on her neck and began passionately laying kisses on her. Mistress Chevalier shushed her, reaching out and placing a silencing finger on Amber's lips.

"No. No format titles tonight my sweet. Tonight, you may call me Jade, provided you remember that you are still here to do as I need."

"Yes, Mis... I mean, yes, Jade," Amber replied. Jade smiled and drew in close, her lips pressing against Amber's mouth and her hand gently cupping her breast.

The kiss was a work of art, conducted on the raw clay of Amber's young, lesbian body by a maestro who had been learning new skills for as long as the younger woman had been alive.

Vicky's hungry mouth against her neck and shoulder was soon matched by the proprietorial fingers which claimed Amber's sex, pushing insistently inside her and thrusting to claim her, as a powerful thumb worked in circles on her aching clit.

Amber gasped into Jade's mouth as her clit was stimulated and then pinched hard by the sadistic older submissive. When Jade's mouth dropped to suck and lick at the nipple she had been lightly fondling with her hand, it all became too much and Amber reached the first of many orgasms.

Jade looked up at her young student, her eyes locking with

Amber's as she hungrily chewed and sucked at the succulent treat between her lips. Amber gasped and bucked on Vicky's strong fingers as both women continued to assault her senses with measured control.

It was mere moments later that their practice movements forced a second orgasm from her willing body and Amber felt her head flush with the intense rush of her climax, it was as if she might faint for a moment but she rode it all the way home.

"Good girl," Jade murmured, pausing from stimulating Amber's engorged nipple for a moment. "Would you like me to eat your pussy, darling?" she asked, a note of playful desire in her voice, as if she was genuinely worried the answer might be in the negative.

"Mmm. Please. Please Jade, lick my cunt, she needs you," Amber begged, putting a hand boldly on the older woman's head and pushing gently toward her crotch.

The thrill of the mighty Mistress Chevalier taking the forceful guidance and descending rapidly down Amber's body, laying a trail of kisses until her tongue finally plunged between Amber's pussy lips, was intense. It felt almost as if she was the one in charge.

Vicky's hand was displaced and reached up to take possession of her left breast, as her other hand snaked under Amber's ribs and grasped her right breast roughly squeezing it before withdrawing as she changed their position..

Vicky rolled Amber onto her back, twisting her until she, still on her side, could lock lips with the younger woman, as their domme began to worship her pussy. The muscular subs tongue thrust into Amber's mouth and claimed her entirely for the whole time it took Jade to bring Amber to another orgasm, which she did far more slowly than Amber imagined she was capable of.

Jade was a self-described connoisseur of pussy and enjoyed savouring such moments, as she'd told Amber several times. Taking her time was her right as a dominant of course, and Amber hardly resented the slow build to such a powerful orgasm as she ended up having, although if it had gone on much longer, she might have changed her tune and begun begging for relief.

As it was, she almost dislodged Jade's hungry mouth as it licked and sucked on her swollen nub, when the orgasm the older woman had drawn from her, made her hips shudder violently and her scream out, "Jade! Oh, Jade!"

But Jade did not stop, did not relent, did not give her any ease for her sensitive pussy, she just kept on tormenting her with the ease of many years of practice. It was as if Amber's pussy was laid out like a grand piano and Jade was a concert pianist who could bring forth Rachmaninov from any keyboard she was presented with, no matter the subtle differences it might have.

Jade may have told Amber to drop her nom de guerre of Mistress Chevalier but she was still firmly in charge of their play tonight. She was an experienced lesbian who had a couple of decades or more of practice at bringing eager sluts like Amber to the brink of ruin with her tongue. Every ounce of that skill was brought to bear on Amber's pussy forcing orgasms from her with a seeming lack of effort.

The grip on Amber's thighs was vice-like in intensity, as Jade's powerful arms denied Amber any chance of escaping her agile tongue. Amber's clit was on fire, her lips swollen and puffy from nibbling, sucking and just plain arousal. She whimpered and cried out, "Please, no more." Still, Jade did not relent. Amber knew there was no reason for her to do so, and her safeword was there for a reason. It had almost begun to bubble from her lips when what could have been her fourth orgasm tore from her aching cunt.

Jade laughed, despite the gush of Amber's first ejaculation, the liquid splashed over her domme's face as she completely lost control. Jade reached out and took hold of Vicky's hair, bringing her close. The athletic submissive knew what was needed of her and began to lick her domme's face clean of Amber's juices. The two women kissed and fondled each other until Jade was satisfied.

Jade stood up and smiled down at Amber, "You've made such a mess of me, Amber, even Vicky's tongue hasn't been able to clean me up. I'm going to wash up. Vicky, get over her face."

Their domme watched as Vicky rose up and squatted over Amber's face, "Yes, now Amber, you have until I come back from freshening up to give Vicky a nice big orgasm. If you don't, I'm going to spank your pussy, understood."

"Yes, Jade," Amber breathed, as Vicky's inviting sex came down to meet her welcoming lips.

Amber worked as hard and fast as she could, and Vicky was thoroughly excited by all the play beforehand, so she felt she might have a chance to avoid an intimate spanking, if Jade's wash was anything more than cursory.

Vicky wasn't making it hard, letting Amber have access to every part of her sex, and before the taps in the en-suite bathroom turned off, she had quietly gushed her orgasm all over Amber's face. It wasn't as explosive as Amber's had been but it was undeniable that Vicky had reached a climax.

Jade emerged from the bathroom, while Vicky was still riding Amber's face. They had not been told to stop if Vicky orgasmed so they had continued. "Well, did she make you come yet, slut?"

Vicky's powerful thighs twitched momentarily and Amber thought she'd lift herself up, but then they clamped on her head, her pussy pressing down hard on her mouth, pausing her ability to breathe and muffling her voice.

"No, Mistress," Vicky said with a shake of her head Amber could feel from beneath her. "I didn't come."

"I'm disappointed, Amber, so disappointed you couldn't be bothered to work your tongue hard enough. I simply must spank your naughty little cunt now. I like to stick to my promises," Jade explained, before kneeling between Amber's widespread legs.

The first smack landed on Amber's pussy without warning as Vicky's powerful frame and tight grip obstructed her vision. Amber howled into Vicky's pussy. Jade laughed loudly at the muffled noise.

"Goodness, Vicky, how tightly have you got hold of her? The poor girl can barely breathe."

"I want my orgasm, Mistress," Vicky growled, grinding her hips into Amber's face.

"You'd better give it to her, Amber, or you'll pass out from lack of oxygen," Jade warned. "I'll speed up your punishment to incentivise you," she added generously.

Counting out each blow, as Amber furiously licked at Vicky's pussy trying to get her to come again, Jade delivered five more hard smacks on Amber's sensitive sex. Each cupped her pussy perfectly, spreading the impact across the mound of wet flesh and making a tremendously satisfying noise.

It was pure agony, but Amber wasn't going to use her safe signal to avoid it. It wasn't for this. Her thighs were soaked with her own arousal and her mind was concentrating hard on bringing Vicky off so she could just about cope with it, though it was going to sting like the blazes for hours.

Amber felt she was almost blue in the face by the time she forced Vicky to come in front of Jade. When Vicky rolled off to one side, shuddering with exhaustion, Amber tried to suck in deep lungfuls of air as quickly as possible. Jade lunged forward and purred, "I want to taste her on you, slut."

Then Amber's airway was restricted again as Jade's lips pressed to hers and their tongues intertwined. Breathing through her nose calmed the panic she'd been feeling as Vicky rode her face in that suffocating style and Jade made appreciative noises as if she was enjoying a delightful new dessert.

Finally, Jade sat back, "That was fun."

"She cheated, Jade. I made her come before you got out here," Amber finally protested, cross to have been punished for Vicky's lie.

"Is that true, Vicky?"

"Yes, it is true, Mistress," Vicky confirmed without apparent shame. "I wanted to come twice and see this beautiful sluts pussy turn bright pink from being spanked."

"I can hardly blame you for that, but you must still be punished of course. Amber, how do you want to do it?" Jade asked.

"Me?"

"Yes, you, have you been squeezed so hard you went deaf?" Jade said, rolling her eyes.

"I think you should spank her pussy too, Jade," Amber said, feeling emboldened.

"No. Not to the pussy spanking, but I want to watch you give out this punishment. I'm supposed to be training you for Susanna. This is a chance for you to learn a pussy torture she might have use for," Jade explained, motioning for Vicky to lie back.

The big submissive did as she was told, lying back and spread her legs wide, putting a pillow under her bottom to lift her hips up and expose her shaven pussy even more. Vicky didn't seem in the slightest concerned about the punishment she was about to receive at the hands of her victim, if anything Amber thought she seemed excited.

"No, no, no! That's not nearly hard enough. You need to bring tears to her eyes, girl," Jade said after Amber had delivered three rather feeble smacks which didn't even make Vicky flinch, let alone wince or cry out.

"Watch me do it," Jade ordered, bringing her hand down with a resounding echo of flesh meeting flesh. Vicky whimpered. "Like that, see?"

"Yes, Jade," Amber said.

Jade nodded and took hold of her hand, showing hers alongside it. "Shape your hand like this, now, feel how it cups her pussy? It's like clapping your hands. Flat together there's barely any noise, and it can hurt you. But cup them, and you can make much louder noises, which for our purposes can be exhilarating in itself, and hit harder without injuring yourself. Just like this," Jade said, bringing her slightly cupped hand down viciously on Vicky's pussy.

Vicky squealed in pain, mixed with thick lust. She was utterly at Amber's mercy as Jade lined up her hand like a golf pro teaching how to hit a ball properly. Jade swung her hand up and down a couple of times and then gave her the nod. "Now, you try again and put some effort into it!"

Amber licked her lips nervously and brought her hand down, almost wincing herself before it connected. There was an echoing slap and Vicky cried out. It felt less painful to her hand and when she lifted her hand away, Amber was pleased to see Vicky's skin flushing pink.

"Yes. Now eleven more like that. Quick as you can," Jade instructed.

"Eleven! She only got six!" Vicky protested.

"Because Amber is a good girl, not a naughty orgasm thief like you, Vicky," Jade chided her. She threw a stern glance at Amber and motioned for her to continue.

As Amber's hand descended time after time, Jade counted out each stroke, docking a couple as mis-hits that didn't land properly which caused further mumbled complaints from Vicky.

"That's better. I think we should practise this again tomorrow at some point. You'd like that, wouldn't you, Vicky," Jade said with a grin.

"Yes, Mistress Chevalier," Vicky said.

"Now, while Vicky is taking a richly deserved punishment, how much nipple torture have you tried, Amber? Would you like to learn how to torment a nipple properly?" Jade asked with a suggestive wiggle of her eyebrows which made Amber giggle.

"Yes, please, Jade. I'd like that very much," Amber finally managed to blurt out between fits of laughter.

"I bloody wouldn't," Vicky protested.

"Then you should be a good girl, Vicky," Jade said, shuffling up the bed, and slinging her leg over Vicky's head so she could press her pussy to her submissive's mouth, as she faced back down the bed at Amber, beckoning her forward.

"Eat me, slut," Jade ordered casually, as she guided Amber's hand to Vicky's nipple. "Now, pinch it, as hard as you can."

Amber did her best but even after several practices it wasn't hard enough for Jade's liking.

"Right, you're doing this all wrong, Amber. Vicky is really much too experienced to respond the way we want if you are so gentle with her."

"I'm squeezing really hard," Amber protested.

Jade shook her head as she rolled her hips over Vicky's wicked tongue. "No, you just think you are because your nipples are more sensitive. You need to learn to judge your partners better. Vicky is a vicious sadist, but she's also a masochist which is why she loves to be on her knees for me. She loves the way I hurt her and make her serve me. But she's tough as old nails to go with it, so what might make Sugar or Candy howl, or you use your safeword won't put a dent in her, do you understand?"

"Yes, Jade," Amber said, trying to comprehend the lesson.

"Pinch her hard then and hold it. Hard as you like," Jade suggested.

Amber reached out and took Vicky's nipple between her thumb and the knuckle of her forefinger, pinching really hard. Vicky did not cry out.

"Good now hold it and watch me," Jade said. "This is what you're doing," she said, demonstrating on Vicky's other nipple.

"Yes, Jade."

"Whereas this is what I'm doing," Jade said, pinching harder, which caused Vicky to shudder. Amber felt the woman's hips, which she was straddling to get access to her big breasts, buck slightly under her. A clear reaction to the infliction of pain by Jade. "See how her nipple is squeezed more in my hand? Tighten your grip so they match," Jade prompted.

Amber did as she was told, applying more pressure than she was comfortable with, trying to get the nipple she was pinching into the same distorted shape as the one Jade had taken control of. A shudder running through Vicky's body between Amber's thighs told her she was onto something.

"Yes, like that," Jade said. "Now, tug it upwards like this. A bit more, that's better. Now, turn your hand clockwise and twist it. Twist it like you're going to pull it off!"

Amber swallowed hard and copied Jade's motions. When they both did it at once, Vicky's muffled cries could be heard blasting into Jade's pussy as it ground against her mouth.

"I did it!" Amber blurted out excitedly.

"Yes you did," Jade said, leaning forward and pulling Amber into a passionate kiss which she kept going until Vicky finally brought her to her orgasm.

Jade broke the kiss to gasp for air as she rode the waves of her climax. Amber hugged her tightly, stroking her hair and kissing her neck as she came down from the rush.

"Is she still licking you, Jade?" Amber asked. Jade pulled back from their embrace and smiled.

"Of course," Jade said. "Vicky is a good girl and never stops licking until she's told to. Are you ready for another lesson?"

Amber nodded. "Yes."

"Good girl," Jade said with a wicked grin. "Slap her tits then."

Amber looked down at Vicky's already tormented breasts. "Slap them?"

"Yes. Swat them and see how she responds. Go on," Jade urged.

Amber looked down and bit her lip for a moment, hesitating. Jade waved her hand in a rolling motion indicating she should press on and Amber slapped her hand against Vicky's breast.

"Again," Jade urged her on. "Again. Harder."

Amber slapped her again and Jade sighed in exasperation.

"I don't want to hurt her too badly," Amber whined.

Jade lifted her pussy from her submissive's face for a moment and asked, "Vicky, is Amber slapping your tits too hard?"

"Is she slapping them, I hadn't noticed, Mistress," Vicky said.

Jade gave Amber a look that firmly said, 'I told you so!' and parked her pussy on Vicky's tongue again.

Amber took a deep breath and slapped again.

"Better, but I want her tits to go the same pink as your bottom does when you get a good, hard spanking from Pudding or Susanna," Jade clarified. "Keep going.

Amber slapped Vicky's breasts a few more times each side. Then Jade lashed her hand out, slapping Amber's left breast hard. Amber squealed in shock and pain. "Ow, what was that for?" she asked, plaintively.

"To teach you an object lesson. At least that hard please," Jade said.

Amber frowned and let rip. There was a much louder sound this time and Vicky's hip bucked under her.

"Much better. Six like that to each of her tits, quick as you can, Amber!" Jade ordered.

Amber complied, much more readily this time and had to switch hands to get the right motion in. By the end of it, her palms were stinging and Vicky was writhing under her like a horse trying to buck a rider. But she didn't use her safe signal or cry out a safeword, despite the shade of hot pink that her breasts were rapidly going.

"Wasn't that fun, Amber?" Jade grinned as she rode Vicky's face to another orgasm of the back of watching Amber inflict the kind of pain she enjoyed doling out herself. The domme panted heavily as she came down from her climax.

"Yes, Jade."

"You can call me Mistress again now," Jade said as she dismounted Vicky's face.

"Yes, Mistress," Amber said.

"Now, get between my legs and lick me until I fall asleep," Jade ordered.

"Yes, Mistress Chevalier," Amber said as she dipped her head to comply.

"Vicky, fuck her from behind with a strap-on, there's a dear," Mistress Chevalier ordered.

"Yes, Mistress," came the cheerful response.

CHAPTER 12

"This morning," Mistress Chevalier told the assembled staff of the estate, "and this afternoon, we will be holding a series of races. This is the final stage of Amber's ponygirl bootcamp week, and will test her new skills."

Amber caught Candy giving her a big wink on the other side of the circle, behind Mistress Chevalier's back. The other women, were concentrating on the Stable Mistress, who had been left in charge while Mistress Susanna was away on business. Amber smiled, but didn't dare wink back or respond to Candy when she should be listening to Mistress Chevalier's speech.

"Each race will award four points for the winner, three for second place and so on down to last place. You will stay in the same teams for the day. The winner will be the ponygirl with the most points at the end of the day," Mistress Chevalier said. "Vicky will be driven by Pudding and I will drive Amber. Ginger will be paired with Sugar and Pepper with Candy. Roxy will be our referee and her decision on points scored and rule infringements will be final. Any questions?"

"Is there a prize, Mistress?" Candy asked.

"For the winning ponygirl, yes. The driver's rewards are built into the format of the races. The winning ponygirl will be allowed to invite

79

anyone here to their bed for the evening, as well as choose who is in charge. Vicky is excluded from winning the grand prize, since she outclasses the other ponygirls in raw power it wouldn't be a fair contest. I still expect everyone to race fairly and attempt to stay as close to Vicky as you can," Mistress Chevalier replied. "There is a treat planned for second place too, the nature of which I will reveal later."

Her answer caused a stir among the teams, as each ponygirl sized up the others, wondering who they could beat and what the second place prize might be. If the winning prize was to fuck whoever they wanted for the night and choose if they were submitting to their choice or vice versa, the second prize could be well worth it too.

"What reward do the drivers get, Mistress Chevalier?" Roxy asked.

"Oh yes, I'm glad you asked. There's not much point trying to race each ponygirl dozens of times, they need to recover after each race or the whole thing will grind to an unbearable mess of glacial speed laps around the lake, like PonyFest 2015. That was a disaster and demonstrated that exhausted ponygirls are far less enjoyable," Mistress Chevalier explained. "To avoid such disappointing events, after each race, the ponygirls will be watered and then will be available for 45 minutes to their drivers. Drivers, you may discipline the ponygirls, use them sexually whatever pleases you, just please keep to the spirit of the event and don't tire them out too much. A tired slut is a boring slut," Mistress Chevalier said. Her last comment caused a small round of laughter.

"You heard Mistress Chevalier, teams! I expect you all ready to race at the starting line by 9am. That means you have," Roxy said, glancing at her fitness band, "twelve minutes, to get in harness and get your traps to the starting line."

Since the girls were already in partial harness and they had already taken the traps out of the coach house, there was plenty of time but Roxy kept in her role as referee and marched around making sure the teams were hustling. She slapped a riding crop against the calf of her thigh-length leather boots, looking for all the world like a posh equestrian girl, out for a day of riding and champagne.

The crack of the crop against the leather of the boot was sharp enough to make Amber flinch every time she heard it, as Mistress Chevalier checked her straps and bit gag, tightening buckles here and there and checking a finger could fit between Amber's skin and the leather of the restraints. Amber knew that was important to prevent loss of blood flow, which could be uncomfortable at best, and caused serious injury at worst.

Once the bit gag was in place, Mistress Chevalier produced a short chain linking two nipple clamps, and attached them to Amber's breasts, causing her eyes to tear up in surprise. Leaning in the domme whispered in Amber's ear, "Just a little something to make sure you remember who is in charge, slut."

The domme reached down between Amber's legs and slipped two fingers between her slick lips, pressing her thumb to Amber's clit. "I knew you'd be wet, you dirty little bitch. Don't forget, the prize you can win if you do well today. If you come last, I'll punish you after each race, understood?"

Amber whinnied and stamped her foot once to indicate she knew very well what was at stake. A full 45 minutes of Mistress Chevalier's cruel punishments would leave her in ruins. She hoped that the alternative if she won was more pleasure than pain, or at least the opportunity to worship her domme rather than be chastised.

"What a good pony. Now, let's see if you can come close to Vicky's pace, shall we?" Mistress Chevalier said as she got in the trap behind Amber and flicked the reins, guiding her to the start line.

The first race got off to a good start, Amber let Pepper and Ginger take off ahead of her and Mistress Chevalier gave her the leeway to choose her own way of racing. Once they passed the first third of the track, Amber increased her pace and used the slight advantage of the shallow incline to overtake both of the more inexperienced ponygirls.

"Well played, Amber," Mistress Chevalier called out as they passed Ginger and Pepper on the left, as they were going clockwise around the lake as usual. Amber wasn't sure if the girls had recognised the terrain changed at this point and became easier, but she was hoping their legs were a little tired from trying to stay far ahead of her. They were huffing and puffing as they tried to catch up with her, but Amber felt fresh enough to keep going and she was gaining ground.

Of course, Vicky was out in front, but Amber didn't let herself worry about that too much. Her first goal was to get more points than Pepper and Ginger, so she could win the prize. She didn't want to burn herself out trying to catch up with Vicky on the first race.

Mistress Chevalier let her set the pace all the way around the end of the lake, then cried out, "Come on Amber, show me you can put in a good finish!"

Amber was planning to move up to a faster gait as she came into the home straight so she kept to her plan as long as she could, almost stumbling when her driver intervened by flicking the carriage whip sharply across her buttocks. The whip cracked, and pain seared Amber's cheeks, "Faster, pony. Faster!"

There was no choice but to do as Mistress Chevalier demanded and try and speed up. Amber was convinced she could not make it and could tell she was going to slow down as her lungs tried hard to provide her with oxygen to keep up her fastest pace. She would be overtaken by one or both of the other ponygirls and come last.

Already, her legs were flagging and Amber, healthy but no athlete, knew she had no reserves to call on for a last burst of speed. Was that the end of her race, she wondered. Then the whip cracked expertly on each buttocks, a split-second apart.

The stinging sensation gave Amber something else to concentrate on and invigorated her with fresh energy, which she put to work in service of her Mistress and drive, Mistress Chevalier.

Amber crossed the line a full hundred yards ahead of Pepper and Ginger's teams.

Mistress Chevalier was already out of the trap and leading her back to the yard when they crossed the finishing line. "Vicky is the winner!" Roxy declared. "Second place goes to Amber, third to Ginger and fourth to Pepper," she called out.

Once the trap was parked, Amber was detached from the rig, and Mistress Chevalier led her into the tack come play room in the stable block. There was no preamble, she unbuttoned her jodhpurs and sat down on a throne-like, well-padded wooden chair before she barked a command at Amber, "Take my boots off."

Amber worked as quickly as possible to get the long boots off so she could remove Mistress Chevalier's riding trousers properly. Without waiting for an order, she got on her knees directly in front of the chair and looked up at Mistress Chevalier, who smiled, pleased that Amber knew her role. The older women shifted forward in the chair, so that her buttocks were balanced on the very edge, making her easy to reach.

"Begin," was the only thing Amber's domme needed to say.

Amber reached out with both hands, teasing aside the lacey scarlet lingerie that concealed Mistress Chevalier's already moist lips with her left hand, and using the fingers of her right to slip between the lips before her and begin fingering her domme. Her tongue followed up immediately, searching for the swollen clit that crowned the delicious pussy of the Stable Mistress.

"Yes, there's a good girl," Mistress Chevalier sighed, as Amber applied her tongue to what had become one of her favourite activities. Behind her, she could hear the other teams following suit.

"Over my knee please, Vicky," Pudding said. Amber knew what that meant. Pudding's world revolved around cooking delicious food and looking after the diet of the staff and guests at Susanna's mansion and spanking women. The cook loved to turn a girl's bottom rosy pink and was so expert, that she could make some girls come just from the way she spanked them. Indeed, it wasn't long before Vicky was moaning and breathing hard, just like Ginger was.

While Pudding's hand descended time after time on Vicky's bottom, Amber had heard Sugar order Ginger to help her into a strap-on harness and begin fucking the ponygirl. She wished that she could see the maid fucking her pony, but the sounds that filled the room were still quite arousing. Mistress Chevalier was adding her own appreciative noises to the atmosphere.

Candy meanwhile, had different ideas, "I'm going to make you come so hard, Pepper and you're going to beat Amber in the next race for me, aren't you?" Amber could hear Pepper's familiar moans as Candy got work licking the lucky ponygirl's pussy.

"Yes, Candy, I can beat her. Oh, that's good. Thank you Mistress," Candy moaned.

Mistress Chevalier was completely relaxed, her eyes closed and her hands stroking her breasts through her blouse, as Amber hungrily tongued and sucked at her clit. "Do you hear that, Amber? Candy thinks she can beat you. You're not going to let her, are you?"

"No, Mistress," Amber replied, taking just a second to speak before going back to worshipping the ponygirl trainer's pussy.

"I hope not, I want to come before Pepper, and I want to win the next race too," Mistress Chevalier said.

The cry that came from Pepper's lips confirmed that Candy had heard that challenge and was redoubling her effort. Amber did too, plunging her fingers into her domme's hungry pussy and finding her g-spot, as she concentrated on her clit with her tongue.

If Amber had to choose, Candy was probably the submissive who was beast at eating pussy, that Mistress Susanna had in service to her, although Mistress Chevalier was amazing as well. The domme had the unfair advantage of having been practicing the most delightful art since before some of them were born.

There was no circumstance under which Amber would have given anything but her all to try and beat Candy. She was determined to be the first to give her partner an orgasm. It wasn't a surprise when Pepper began to scream her way through an epic orgasm, a full minute before Amber got the same from Mistress Chevalier.

The reaction to the climax that Mistress Chevalier experienced still made Amber proud. She didn't expect to beat Candy at pussy eating, or Vicky at racing yet but she was pleased with her progress. Everyone else in the room had been having sex with other women far longer than she had, after all.

Mistress Chevalier however, wasn't going to leave it at Amber having been defeated. When she was done, she reached for a wet wipe and made herself decent, pulling up her trousers and having Amber help her get her riding boots on.

Then she bent Amber over a spanking bench and thrashed her a dozen times with a flogger. With expert aim, she made it sting just the right amount to discipline her submissive, but not enough that Amber couldn't go through the rest of the day. Already, Amber could tell she wouldn't be able to see evidence of the pain she'd just suffered if she looked in the mirror.

Amber wanted to come so badly then, but Mistress Chevalier wasn't looking to please the sub, she was keen to get on with the day of racing.

Pepper had obviously been encouraged by the orgasmic bribe that Candy gave her, and she beat Amber and Ginger in the next race. Although Amber's trick from the first race wasn't going to work again, she found that an even pace, and paying attention to Mistress Chevaliers commands, both verbal and with the reins, worked well.

By the end of the day, Vicky had comfortably won each race, winning sixteen points. Pepper won the second round but lost the third and only beat Ginger in the fourth race earning eight points in total. Ginger was last with only seven points.

"Amber wins second place, with ten points overall," shouted Roxy at the end of the last race.

The ponygirls were all good sports and cheered her on.

Mistress Chevalier pulled her in for a long kiss, and fondled Amber's bottom while she claimed her trainee's mouth for some long, passionate moments.

"Good girl," she said, "now, you are due a prize. Who do you wish to take to bed tonight?" Mistress Chevalier waved her hand to indicate the assembled women that Amber could choose from.

"Can I pick more than one?" Amber asked, fluttering her eyelashes at the Stable Mistress.

"I suppose you can, you naughty minx, I didn't say it had to be just one girl, so it's not against the rules."

"I'd like all the ponygirls to join me in bed then, so we can please each other all night long. And you, of course, Mistress."

"Well, of course. How thoroughly greedy of you, Amber," Mistress Chevalier said with a sly smile.

"Yes, Mistress. I am a very greedy girl I've discovered since coming here. I love to eat as often as I can," Amber replied.

"What about Pudding and Sugar and Candy?"

"Would it be alright if they stayed to watch? I'm sure Sugar and Candy have done something naughty that requires Pudding to punish them," Amber suggested.

"Have they done anything requiring punishment, Pudding? Anything naughty?" Mistress Chevalier asked the cook.

"They've always got a black mark against their name. They're a lot of trouble you know, Mistress?" Pudding replied. "I have a list, if you wish to see it."

Mistress Chevalier laughed heartily, "No, but make sure you make them squeal, won't you? It wouldn't do for them to think they can have too many punishments without crying some cathartic tears, wouldn't you agree?"

"Of course, Mistress. The maids need to be kept firmly in their place at the bottom of our social ladder. You can't give them an inch or they'll take a mile," Pudding agreed. "I'll be sure to leave them tear-streaked and with blushing bottoms."

"Good then, it's settled. Ladies, to bed," Mistress Chevalier ordered. "Roxy, you too."

"Yes, Mistress," the seven submissive women chorused.

CHAPTER 13

"Congratulations, Amber, you did so well," Candy said.

"Yes, well done," Sugar said, giving her a big hug.

"You need to do more squats, short stuff," Vicky said before pulling her in for a bear hug that Amber thought might crush her.

"I'm sure Mistress Susanna will offer you a stall of your own, Amber," Pepper whispered in her ear as she and Ginger enveloped her in a shared hug.

"I bet you're right, Pepper," Ginger agreed.

"Thanks ladies," Amber said when everyone finally stopped congratulating her for passing Mistress Susanna's battery of tests. It felt good to have mastered the skills that Mistress Chevalier had spent many long hours teaching her, at least well enough to be considered competent. It was like passing a driving test or getting a swimming certificate that proved you were a good enough swimmer to be safe on your own.

The difference was that Amber was torn up inside. She'd had a certain amount of fun, but she was worried about what would happen next. As they worked on putting away all the traps and harnesses properly and all got showered together, Amber mulled things over in her mind.

What was it that she wanted from Mistress Susanna, now that she was back?

When Susanna had seduced her just a few short weeks ago, Amber's life had gone from what could only be described as rather uneventful, to a thrilling sequence of incredible sexual and romantic adventures.

For all intents and purposes she was the girlfriend of a wealthy business woman now, and even the thought of being a lesbian was new to her. Amber's inexperience with women before she met Susanna wasn't just due to a lack of opportunity, it was something she'd never quite settled in her mind, until that fateful moment in her boss's office, during the final interview.

Now she had a new job which had not been taxing so far but could well be quite enjoyable and would certainly offer opportunities that she'd be unlikely to get elsewhere. It wasn't just the sex and the kinky games, but potentially learning a lot about business matters that she couldn't learn elsewhere.

It had been Amber's idea to bring Mistress Chevalier to the estate to run the ponygirl stables, operate her business as a leatherworker there and renovate more of the outbuildings to accomplish that. Amber had expected the idea to be rejected outright, but Susanna gave her the responsibility of overseeing the whole thing.

Certainly, she hadn't had to do anything alone and had required lots of help, but Susanna had let her remain in charge and instead of dictating how it would go, had offered suggestions along the way. Amber had learned a lot about property investment, bookkeeping, project management and a host of other valuable business skills.

Most employers and managers, wouldn't be given so much rope to an employee at such a young age. If she hadn't also been her boss's lover, her self-doubting said from one shoulder, perhaps it wouldn't have gone the same way. Her confidence shouted from the other shoulder, that she was still learning a lot, even if it was only because she was sleeping with Susanna.

Was it a tick in the pro column or the con column that Amber's boss was an older woman who had quite deliberately headhunted a beautiful young woman, to be her personal assistant, in the hopes that she'd also fit in with her hedonistic lifestyle?

Did it matter if Amber's employment opportunities were in part coming to her because Susanna enjoyed dominating her, disciplining her rosy cheeked bottom, and riding her face to orgasm? If it wasn't all about Amber's abilities as an employee, was that a point of principal that should cause Amber to reject the marvellous opportunities that Susanna offered. Doing so would probably mean rejecting the older woman romantically as well.

It just didn't feel to Amber that she was doing anything wrong. Her feelings for Susanna were new, but genuine. Although she'd never been past the fantasy stage of thinking about sex with another woman, there wasn't a shred of doubt that she was attracted to them.

The sex was amazing and Amber was coming to terms with how much she enjoyed being submissive to Susanna, Mistress Chevalier and anyone they told her to. The kinky games and BDSM that they indulged in were sometimes humiliating, sometimes painful but always arousing and ultimately fulfilling.

The orgies that Amber had now been a part of, were so decadent that she felt she should somehow feel guilty about being so sexually open and giving. And yet, Amber experienced nothing she could identify as a guilty thought for more than a second or two. Each hint of another event where Amber might enjoy group sex or get shared with Mistress Susanna's friends, left her wet with anticipation, not scared or disgusted.

Amber had been hoping that when Susanna got back, another project would come up that would allow her to prove her worth to her Mistress in the business, and not just the bedroom. Did Susanna really respect her opinions or was she simply indulging her pet's interest to keep her happy?

A nagging doubt remained, though Amber felt that it was entirely rational to think Susanna really did want to listen to her ideas. It was unlike any management style Amber had experienced herself and more the stuff of books about entrepreneurs and the opportunities their boss's had given them.

While her mind raced with the complexities of her current situation she and the other ladies had all got dressed and were heading toward the house for dinner. A part of Amber hoped it would devolve into another lesbian orgy of the senses, a hedonistic night of pleasure, pain and laughter. If not, perhaps she would be able to grab a moment to speak to Susanna about her future.

"Come on Amber, keep up!" Candy urged.

"I'm right behind you," Amber said, though she could feel herself hesitating, her anxiety about her life going forward was distracting her. She shook her head and took a deep breath.

Amber stepped through the door into the rest of her life.

CHAPTER 14

"Ladies, a moment of your time. Ladies, your attention please!" Susanna said, tapping a knife on the side of her glass to get their attention.

The chatter around the dining table finished and everyone turned their eyes toward their employer and Mistress.

"Thank you."

Mistress Susanna smiled at them all and put the knife down, lifting her glass of wine.

"Please raise your glasses for a toast," Susanna asked, "To Amber, our new friend, colleague and filthy slut!"

"To Amber," the ladies laughed.

"I know that you've all enjoyed having Amber her at the estate and you've all felt the pleasure of her tongue on your pussies. I'm sure you agree that she's come along nicely so far and of course, today, she passed her final exam from the Mistress Chevalier school of teaching dirty girls to be good ponygirls," Susanna continued to politely laughter.

"In other news, we may need to have a brainstorming session for a better name for the school," Mistress Susanna said, and had to wait for the laughter to quiet down.

"Amber, when I first interviewed you, which seems like it was only last week, I was pleased to offer you a job as my personal assistant. You've performed your duties admirably and learned so much about yourself since you came to live here. I'm immensely proud of you, as I am of all the wonderful ladies around this table. We are a team bonded on so many levels," Mistress Susanna said.

"Hear, hear!" agreed Mistress Chevalier boisterously.

"You passed the exams Mistress Chevalier, and I set, proving that you paid attention during her lessons and have demonstrated you have the capability to make a good ponygirl. I would like to offer you the position of ponygirl alongside Pepper and Ginger in my stables, as I feel you've earned it. What do you say?"

Amber's eyes flew wide, and she glanced around the table at all the women smiling at her. Her heart beat furiously in her chest and she could feel them staring at her, all at once.

Mistress Susanna was smiling at her waiting for a response, but as the seconds ticked by without Amber replying, her smile began to crack at the corners. Amber swallowed and licked her lips. She knew she had to say something and didn't think her answer was going to please her Mistress. There was no choice though.

"Thank you, Mistress. That's a kind offer, but I will have to decline I'm afraid."

The room erupted with gasps of shock, hands flew to mouths and murmurs grew loud around her. Amber felt herself shrinking into her seat as oddly loud whispered conversations took place.

"Calm down! Calm down! Please be quiet so I can ask Amber about this," Mistress Susanna called out over the gossipers. "Amber, you have taken to being a ponygirl rather well, and by all accounts you had an enjoyable week of roleplaying and fun. Therefore, I must ask why you would turn this down. Do we need to discuss this in private?"

Amber nodded, "Yes, please, Mistress."

Susanna sighed, "Then please, join me in the drawing room. Ladies, please amuse yourselves while I talk to Amber."

The chattering started up again and gained full throated involvement by the time Mistress Susanna closed the door behind them.

Mistress Susanna sat down on a leather Chesterfield, and motioned for Amber to come forward and sit astride her, her knees sinking into the soft, burgundy leather, as she kneeled in her Mistress's lap. Susanna's eyes roved appreciatively up and down Amber's nubile body, drinking in her shapely form.

Reaching out, Mistress Susanna slipped the thin straps of Amber's dress off her shoulders and revealed her breasts. Amber took a deep breath as her lover began to stroke her breasts and tease her nipples. It was several minutes before Mistress Susanna deigned to speak to her, but her domme did not stop fondling her breasts.

"I'm not going to make this easy on you, Amber. You can explain your rejection of my offer but I haven't seen you in so long, I have no intention of not enjoying your lovely breasts while you do so," Mistress Susanna purred. "Please, enlighten me."

The damp patch in Amber's lacy panties wasn't helping her concentrate, but she managed to pull together her thoughts sufficiently to respond without resorting to lust induced gibberish.

"I did my best to be a good ponygirl, Mistress, and it's true, I had a fun week in some regards. I just can't see myself living like Pepper and Ginger do long term," Amber explained whimpering slightly as Mistress Susanna pinched her nipples most cruelly. When she'd recovered she went on, "I don't want to be your ponygirl, Mistress."

"No? Then what do you want, Amber?"

"I want to be you, Mistress."

"You want to be me? Figuratively, I hope, otherwise you'll have a difficult road ahead of you."

"I want to be a strong, independent business woman, like you, Mistress. I want to learn how to grow a business and shape some portion of the world the way you have. I could do so much good in the world, if I take this wonderful opportunity to learn everything you have to teach. One day, I could own my own company or run a foundation or make a contribution to the world. With your guidance, with you as my mentor, I think I can do it."

Mistress Susanna's hands dropped away from Amber's breasts and she looked upset.

"I see. You want to end our relationship and go into business for yourself? It makes sense I suppose, you got a taste of it with the renovation project and now you want more. I can hardly criticise you for that," Mistress Susanna said, sounding as dejected as if someone had just told her that her favourite restaurants had all closed shop permanently.

"No!" Amber protested.

"No? Is that all I'll get from you now, a negative response to everything?" Mistress Susanna grumbled.

"No, Mistress. I mean, I don't want to end our relationship. I don't want that at all. I want to be your personal assistant and learn about business at your side. But I still want you, I want to serve you. I just don't want to do it as a ponygirl or have it be so much of every day of my life."

"So you just want to share my bed, as long as there's some kind of business coaching for you?"

Amber shook her head. "I want to share your bed because I want to worship you, for the goddess you are to me, Mistress Susanna."

Mistress Susanna was still frowning, her arms crossed defensively in front of her.

Amber reached out her hand and tilted her dommes chin up, forcing her to look her in the eye. It was a bold move, and Amber could already picture being bent over and thrashed soundly for daring to be so forward.

"Mistress. I..." Amber trailed off.

"You what?" Mistress Susanna said, glaring into Amber's very soul.

"Mistress, you know that I love you, don't you? You know that every moment apart this week has been agony for me, far beyond the torments that Mistress Chevalier inflicted. I don't want to be in the stables. I want to be in your bed. I want to wake up next to you. When you invite Candy to your bed and have her lick your delicious pussy, I want to be beside you, watching my love receive her pleasure."

"You love me? Really, truly, love me?"

"Yes, Mistress. Haven't I shown that?"

"But you won't be my ponygirl?"

"Susannna, do you really need another ponygirl? Honestly?"

"I don't need one," Susanna said, almost whining and placing greater emphasis on the penultimate word. "I don't see why I can't have another one.

Amber rolled her eyes and giggled. "Very well, Mistress. As soon as I get the chance, I shall set myself a project, 'Find greedy Mistress Susanna a third ponygirl. Must have big boobs, pierced nipples and a craving for more discipline in her life.' How's that?"

Mistress Susanna laughed. "It'd be nice if she had some tattoos, and tongue and clit piercings too," she joked.

"I'll make a note of it. 'Pierced everywhere. Only genuine sluts need apply.'" Amber replied solemnly.

"Perfect. You know, you'd probably make a good personal assistant, Amber," Susanna said with a wink.

"That's what I've been saying!" Amber giggled. Susanna's hands found her breasts again and Amber's nipples were soon as stiff as bullets, or at least, as she imagined bullets must be, not that she'd ever held one. "Oh, Mistress. That feels wonderful."

"I love you too, Amber."

"I know."

"You did not," Susanna said, looking faintly scandalised

"I think I did."

"Did you just quote that scruffy scoundrel?" Susanna said, shaking her head softly as Amber's hands reached out and gently stroked her breasts through her dress.

"You know I did." Amber replied, rubbing her thumbs over her domme's hardening nipples.

"I happen to like nice girls," Susanna said, emphasising her words with a cruel, twisting pinch of Amber's nipples.

"No, you don't," Amber gasped, her eyes watering as she leaned in to claim her Mistress's mouth with a passionate kiss, as her fingers played down her stomach and slid into her panties. Susanna did not protest Amber contradicting her.

The wet lips her fingers slipped between would have borne out her statement, regardless. Mistress Susanna tipped her head back and moaned her confession.

"Yes, Amber."

CHAPTER 15

Amber had wanted to ravish Susanna right there and then, but her Mistress and boss would not allow her to take it quite that far. She insisted they tidy themselves up and get back to the dinner party. Amber tried pouting, but it simply earned her a rather casual smack across the rump and a stern look which further dampened her panties but didn't lead to any more fooling around.

Mistress Susanna did lift Amber's fingers to her lips and suck them clean of her own juices, winking lasciviously at Amber as she did so. "Mmm. I do taste good, don't I?"

"Yes, Mistress," Amber breathed, utterly enraptured by the horny display.

"Now, we must go back to the others, I want to speak to them about what we've discussed."

"You do?"

"I do, come along now," Mistress Susanna said, taking Amber's hand in hers and leading her back to the formal dining room with its large banquet table surrounded by all the household staff, from Roxy and Pudding to the ponygirls and Mistress Chevalier and the maids.

Normally they did not all eat together, and the maids ate with the cook, but Amber passing her exams was a major event and Mistress

Susanna had decreed it a celebration. Pudding had cooked an amazing meal and once it was served, the cook and maids had joined the rest of the household.

The room was full of conversation when the doors opened and quieted down quickly when Mistress Susanna strode in with Amber in tow.

"Ladies, I have an announcement to make, Amber has decided against the life of a ponygirl and I was surprised, but I fully support her reasoning. I'm pleased to say that she will continue to serve as my personal assistant and live here with us," Mistress Susanna said.

The assembled ladies clapped and cheered happily.

"I know that some of you probably hoped Amber would want to play as a pony with you, but I'm sure you'll have plenty of fun with her regardless of that," Susanna said. Mistress Chevalier agreed loudly.

"I'd like you all to follow me to the sitting room," Susanna said, striding from the dining room into a nearby room which was set up with lots of comfy chairs and chaise longue, a baby grand piano in one corner. It was a grandly appointed room and one of the main rooms used during the orgy a few weeks previously.

Susanna had them clear the coffee tables and Ottomans from the middle of the room, and stand around in a semi-circle while she stood in front of the fireplace with Amber.

"Sugar, please remove Amber's dress and hang it up somewhere neatly," Susanna said calmly as if it were the most natural thing in the world.

"Candy, fetch me the rosewood box in the writing bureau would, my dear?" Susanna said, as Sugar slipped the straps of Amber's elegant dress off her shoulders, and brought it down her body, to puddle around her ankles. Amber stepped out of it and Sugar took the dress away.

Candy had found the expensive looking box, which looked like the type used for expensive diamond jewellery, only that it was an expensive work of art in itself. It was probably an antique, Amber thought.

"Sugar, take her panties too, they're pretty but I think everyone would rather see Amber full nude, am I right, ladies?"

The assembled ladies gave a resounding confirmation and Amber couldn't help but blush, despite the encounters she'd had with each of them, her sense of mild embarrassment at being exhibited for their enjoyment remained. Stepping out of the panties as Sugar worked them down her legs, left her utterly exposed, her neatly shaven pussy on display for all to see.

"Much better," Mistress Susanna said. "I have asked you in here, to bear witness to this moment. Amber, please kneel."

A little murmuring rose up among the ladies but a sharp glance from Susanna brought silence as Amber dropped to the rug on her knees. Amber kept her back straight, and shoulders back, filling her lungs and making sure she was displayed well for her Mistress, and the audience.

"Amber, it is perhaps premature to suggest this, but I would like you to consider doing me the honour of accepting this token," Mistress Susanna said, opening the box and presenting the contents for all, including Amber, to see.

"This is merely a placeholder, a play item I had made for you, in anticipation of this happy moment," Mistress Susanna said. "The real one would be somewhat different and more symbolic," she explained.

Inside the box, on a velvet cushion, lay a beautiful leather collar. It was a deep burgundy, with fine stitching and stamped with beautiful patterns. At the throat there was a silver nameplate that read, "Amber" above a thick half-moon hoop for a leash or restraint. It was very tall, almost neck height. It was a posture collar, she realised, one that would keep the submissives head in a particular position and restrict movement.

"Amber, will you accept my collar, and the commitment that it represents?"

As Susanna had said, this collar was an item for play but collaring a sub was a huge step, tantamount to a proposal of marriage, Amber well knew. None of Susanna's many submissives had been blessed in this way, although they all had a great deal of commitment from Susanna. This was special, unique.

The room was utterly silent, everyone waiting with bated breath on Amber's answer.

Amber felt tears well in her eyes, overwhelmed with the emotional weight of the response she had to give.

"Yes, Mistress."

AUTHOR'S NOTE

Thank you for reading Driven by Her Lesbian Boss, Book Six of the Submissive Lesbian Personal Assistant series.

If you enjoyed the book and can spare the time to leave a review on Amazon or Goodreads, I would greatly appreciate it.

Positive and constructive feedback and comments, even a simple star rating, are a great way to let me know that you want to read more about these characters.

News and Updates - March 2020

Below you'll find some information about this series and the projects I'm working on next. You don't need to read this, but it's here for those who are interested.

Thanks, K.F. Jones

Amber and Susanna

As with Shared by Her Lesbian Boss, you'll find that this book is longer than the first few books, at 27.5K words.

It wasn't intentional but there was a lot more to the fifth and sixth books. You can't have lots of extra characters, orgies and pony girl training without a bit more text.

Last time around, I said I was going to try and keep Driven a bit shorter than Shared but I failed that. I hope you like the book and the extra stuff. There's no extra charge.

I've done another pass on Punished by Her Lesbian Boss, so it will also go from 13.5k to over 17K words. A few niggling errors have been removed so thanks to any reader who submits typos through the Kindle App, it really does help authors.

The first book was 13.5k, the fourth jumped to 17.7k and this one is a whopping 27.4K!

Driven by Her Lesbian Boss is the last book in this series, or, I should say, the last book for the time being. It concludes the main story arc for Amber and Susanna.

I'm really happy to be launching this in March 2020 because I've (only just) hit the target I set in the author notes for Shared.

I'm going to release the box set (titled Her Lesbian Boss: The Complete Box Set), for this series as soon as the cover is done, which will probably be early April.

As I mentioned in my last author notes, I planned to release this omnibus at at the £9.99/$9.99 price point, bought separately in ebook format, all six books would cost £17.94/$17.94. It's a bargain for people who buy directly, and Kindle Unlimited readers can access the book for free anyway.

Instead, I'm going to target the £0.99/$0.99 price point for launch and I may keep it at that low price.

Most of my income from these books comes from Kindle Unlimited subscribers, borrowing and reading them. I'm paid per page read for those readers.

Selling a large box set at a huge discount, will hopefully allow me to reach more readers, push the book higher up the charts and I can then reach more KU readers as a result.

If not, a lot of people will get a very cheap book and I'll raise the price later.

Launching books is a lot of trial and error and the same techniques don't always work.

If price is an issue, the most cost effective way to read my books is to subscribe to Kindle Unlimited (if you read a few a month). That's how I read so much, I could simply never afford to read everything I do, if it I had to buy each book, rather than borrow it.

As I mentioned last time, I really enjoy writing about Amber and Susanna, and I have plenty of ideas as to what they will get up to as their relationship develops. If there is sufficient demand, I'll write another series about their ongoing spankings. I mean, adventures.

Do I hear the cry of tropical birds on an island retreat for kinky lesbians? Perhaps the sound of bells, which could either signal a wedding, or a thoroughly deviant surprise some of our dominants have for their subs?

Remember, let me know what you want, because I promise, I will pay close attention to requests.

You can follow me on Twitter if you want to see every panicked post I make about a new story idea I've had, that I have outlined but don't have time to write.

This happens to me a lot when what I'm really trying to do is get a nice lather of my favourite Tea Tree oil soap all over me in the shower.

One day, I will write some of them.

How to Read the Updated Books

For various reasons, you won't automatically get an updated version of the Punished text, even if you re-download it. I may tweak the text of books 2-3 a bit for the box set (but not as much) and the same applies to those books.

I will ask Amazon to allow people to download the up to date version of Punished, but you also have to go to Manage Content and Devices and confirm you want the upload (because you'll lose any notes or bookmarks in the process, it's not automatic by default).

If you really want to re-read the series with the most up to date versions, you'll soon be able to get the six-book box set edition - Her Lesbian Boss: The Complete Box Set.

If you have Kindle Unlimited you'll be able to borrow it for free, and as it's a new book, you'll only see the new text.

I know, it all sounds a bit complicated but I don't want any of my readers to splash out extra money to read an updated version.

I hope this all makes sense, but you can always reach out to me on Twitter if you are a fan and want to ask questions :)

Amber's Culinary Adventures

I also have plans to write a series of short stories, Amber's Culinary Adventures. Don't worry, they're not actually about cooking. Here's some title ideas - see if they whet your appetite:

- A Dash of Pepper (available now)
- A Sprinkling of Sugar
- A Taste of Pudding
- A Filling of Ginger

The Culinary Adventures will be single scene, erotic shorts about an encounter Amber has with one or more of her friends.

As with A Dash of Pepper, I will release them all as individual works, at the lowest price point Amazon allows, £0.99/$0.99. They will also be available in Kindle Unlimited.

When I have enough, I will release an omnibus which will be the most cost effective way to read the stories if you don't subscribe to Kindle Unlimited.

If you prefer not to buy erotica short stories (this series is made up of novelettes and novellas for anyone who is curious) that's perfectly understandable.

At that price point, they're kind of loss leaders for me anyway due to the way Amazon's royalty structure works (that's not a complaint just something we consider when pricing).

What I expect is for readers to prefer to buy the omnibus edition of short stories instead, but I'll publish them individually too, rather than wait based on that assumption. In any case, the Kindle Unlimited readers can download them one at a time if they exist as individual books.

Here's a summary:

- A series of erotic stories about Amber
- Short, one or two scenes, 5K words
- $0.99/£0.99 individually
- Omnibus to follow
- Seven outlined so far!

One advantage these shorts have, is that I can fit them in as palate cleansers (for me) between other writing projects.

Hellcats Academy - Izzy & Kaos

Carlotta and I will be starting our outlining next week for the revamped Hellcats series, if all goes according to plan at least. We had a virtual (social distancing friendly) meeting this evening to discuss our plans.

Enchanted, our paranormal reverse harem romance about Izzy and Kaos was far too steamy for the average reverse harem/why choose, reader, but also didn't quite satisfy their other requirements either.

We'll be rewriting book one completely. You'll meet the antagonists in that new version. If we'd continued as was, they wouldn't have been featured until later in the series.

Izzy is our main hero and needs to be the centre of attention, from the reader, not just her growing harem of sexy men.

Kaos and her harem will be taking a back seat, rather than playing an equal part in the main series. Kaos will remain in the main series as both a reluctant opponent in the contest, and a valuable ally against the antagonists.

Because I can't help myself, I'll be making sure to detail the life of

Kaos as she recruits, trains, dominates, torments, and otherwise plays with her own harem. We'll release those works as a separate but consecutive erotica series for those of you who want the extra steamy bits and to know more about Kaos (probably).

I can't put a precise timescale on this, particularly during the current problems but you'll be able to see regular updates on my Twitter if you want.

My Twitter is decidedly NSFW (Not Safe For Work) so don't follow me there if that would be problematic for you.

I'm afraid I follow and retweet all sorts of erotica authors, artists, photographers and naughtiness, so you have been warned.

My Facebook is much tamer, aside from the covers which aren't all that risqué anyway.

A note on Kindle Unlimited

I have recently seen a few social media comments from Kindle Unlimited (KU) subscribers who are worried that borrowing a book doesn't help the author they want to support.

I'd like to take a moment to explain why you needn't worry about this. The TLDR (too long, didn't read) version of this is, "Please borrow and read as many books as you want in KU. Don't feel you have to buy them outright to support your favourite authors."

For anyone who wants a bit more details, I'll try and explain this as briefly as possible. Because a KU subscription lets you borrow a book for 'free' I think some readers think the author is not paid at all.

Actually, we get paid per page that you read. Longer books thus earn more for us in KU than shorter ones, and may even earn more from KU reads than the cover price we've set.

Many new authors think that that's a bad deal for us, but if that were true, why are so many great authors putting books in KU?

There are more benefits to us than just the payment per book. Each sale of a book improves our ranking on Amazon. But a borrow is equivalent to a sale.

Rising in the charts, especially into the top 100 for a genre, means our book is seen by more readers. Everything else being equal, if more people see our books, more will buy them or borrow them.

Making a living as an author is simply about having enough readers who regularly choose your books. It doesn't take all that many readers to support the equivalent income of a full-time job.

Speaking only for myself I worry about my readers, my friends and family and their finances. I'm a frugal person, with relatively minimal living expenses. I have a lot of debt and I'm not wealthy, but the future I can see for me, is wonderful. Many people are not so fortunate.

I write full-time (in other genres as well) and my only income is from selling my books.

I would still much rather have someone borrow my book in KU than buy it outright, unless that's their preference. Some of my readers purchase my erotica in paperback format and that's great.

I like paperback books too, but I no longer have to carry them on a train or a plane. My ideal home would essentially be a library with a kitchen and a bathroom, and a big armchair for falling asleep in while reading.

Whether you want to read my books in KU, buy the Kindle, or the paperback, I'm happy to have you as a reader.

I run sales on my books and sometimes put the first in a series up free. Every series I complete will be available in a box set, which will be cheaper for those not using KU.

I do that, because smarter authors than me, have proven it is worthwhile to offer discounts to attract readers.

I just want lots of people to read my books. I'd like to reach the point where I have paid off my debts, have a mortgage and can donate some of my excess income to charities.

It's really touching to me that people are thinking about the authors and other artists they support, and are keen to support us. But don't go hungry or miss a bill doing it, and don't feel bad about being a KU user.

Now, if you recently won an enormous lottery and want to read in KU, then buy the Kindle and the paperback, none of us are going to object. I just don't want to think that someone might spend money they shouldn't for my benefit.

If you want to help more, a **review** on **Amazon** or **Goodreads** is enormously helpful. Not many readers review erotica and I get why but it would be wonderful to have more reviews as it helps other readers choose the right books.

I figure if you're reading my really long author notes, you might be amenable to say something nice, or at least constructive.

I love a glowing review as much as the next author but honesty and constructive criticism are better than flattery.*

If there are any of readers who have been worrying about whether Kindle Unlimited is fair on authors because they get the books 'free' just remember, you pay a subscription, and that's where Amazon gets money to pay us.

If the business model didn't work for readers, Amazon and authors, it would shut down.

With love, KF Jones.

*I am so down for being flattered though.

Let Me Know What You Think

For those of you who have Kindle Unlimited, you can borrow all my books and, if you want to read them again at some point, you'll be able to borrow the omnibus editions so they don't use up lots of slots in your Kindle library.

Don't forget to let me know if you want me to prioritise writing more of the Lesbian Boss series, over say, finishing the Sexy Student Lessons series or adding another quartet to my Consort of the Werewolf King series.

I'm quite active on Twitter at the moment though it's NSFW (not safe for work), so be warned.

It's a pretty good place to reach me as I write this (March 2020) if you want to support me, talk about the books, or let me know which of my series I should concentrate on next.

Thanks for your support, and for buying the book or borrowing it through Kindle Unlimited.

Yours steamily,

K.F. Jones

The Consort of the Werewolf King is the first series by K.F. Jones and follows a young English biology student, who is bitten by a wild wolf.

His friends and colleagues insist that there are no wolves in the UK. William's hunt to prove he was not imagining things leads him to meet, Brian, a local landowner who may be more than he seems.

Consort of the Werewolf King

Bitten by the Alpha - Book 1

Claimed by the Alpha - Book 2

Trained by the Alpha - Book 3

Initiated by the Pack - Book 4

Other work by K.F. Jones

Dawn and the Galvanic Capacitor

Dawn and The Pilferer's Punishment

Dawn and the London Society

Dawn is a bounty hunter, bodyguard and private detective in a steampunk world full of adventure, excitement and lusty antics.

The Tribulations of Dawn will follow our heroine as she tries to reclaim a stolen item for her employer. The Professor is at the forefront of research into advanced steam technology, and his invention could change the world for good or ill.

Dawn has a wandering, and somewhat lascivious eye, to match her quick wit and mean right hook. Woe betide the thieves when she catches them.

But can she be well-behaved for long enough to safely return the gizmo to the Professor? Or will it slip through her fingers and send her off on the chase again?

Submissive Lesbian Personal Assistant

Amber, a young woman who is seduced by her new employer, a dominant and wealthy lesbian.

It is now complete, with a HEA but I may write another follow on if there is demand.

Punished by Her Lesbian Boss

Seduced by Her Lesbian Boss

Trained by Her Lesbian Boss

Raced by Her Lesbian Boss

Shared by Her Lesbian Boss

Driven by Her Lesbian Boss

Her Lesbian Boss: The Complete Box Set

ABOUT THE AUTHOR

K.F. Jones writes erotica and romance books in a range of genres, with the first series, The Consort of the Werewolf King being a paranormal erotic romance.

CotWK is about a young man, Will, who finds love in the arms of Brian, a mature alpha older werewolf with a kinky streak, and a shocking secret. Brian teaches his new cub everything he needs to know to complete his initiation ritual with the pack.

The steampunk world of Dawn, a bold and lusty heroine on a mission to recover a dangerous stolen invention, is an ideal setting for all sorts of sexy, funny, adventures. When time permits, you'll see far more books in this series.

The Submissive Lesbian Personal Assistant series of six books is complete and the box set will be released soon.

The next project is a refreshed version of Enchanted, the first book in the Hellcat Academy setting.

If you'd like to find out when new books are released, join the mailing list at the website. **http://kfjones.net/**

twitter.com/kfjonesauthor

facebook.com/KFJonesbooks

pinterest.com/kfjonesauthor

goodreads.com/kfjones

amazon.com/author/kfjonesbooks